THE RIGHT ANGLE CLUB

Annual Report 2015

Copyright 2015
Printed by Ross & Perry, Inc., 2015
© Ross & Perry, Inc., 2015 on new material. All Rights reserved.
Printed in the United States of America
Ross & Perry, Inc. Publishers
3 South Haddon Avenue, Suite 4
Haddonfield, N.J. 08033
. Telephone (856) 427-6135
Facsimile (856) 427-6136
Visit us at www.rossperry.com
http://www.rossperry.com

ISBN: 978-1-932109-52-8

Book Cover designed by Just Ink

Table of Contents

To see photos in color visit http://www.philadelphia-reflections.com/topic/277.htm

TOPIC 277 Right Angle Club: 2015

Right Angle Club 2015

The Right Angle President Letter: Carter Broach

Clearly, the most momentous event in the 93rd year of the Right Angle Club's existence was the Board of Control's decision to relocate our weekly lunches to The Pyramid Club on the top of the BNY Mellon Bank Center. Reluctantly, we left our home of many years, The Racquet Club, to restore the quality and variety of the lunch menu at an affordable price that members expect.

Anticipating our 100th anniversary, the Board established a Centennial Fund to which members may donate funds voluntarily for the celebration of this event.

I want to thank the officers and board members-at-large for their service to the club. Dan Sossaman, II served as Events Chair, Wayne Strasbaugh was Membership Chair, John Coates was in charge of the Raffle, Mel Buckman served as Recording Secretary and Tom Williams was Treasurer. Frank Bell, Steve Bennett, Stephen Clowery, Bob Hoover, Morris Klein and Ted Laws were the Boards' Members-at-Large.

I especially appreciate the tremendous job Chad Bardone did as Speaker Chair. By common consent, the Speaker Chair is the most demanding position in the club. He recruits speakers for about 75% of the lunches in a year, hosts the speakers at our lunches, takes care of the speakers' audio-visual equipment needs and introduces speakers to the club. Chad never failed to deliver.

While officers and Board members serve limited terms, our Treasurer, Tom Williams, continues *ad infinitum*. He is the financial guru who invoices members for dues, collects and deposits their payments, pays the club's bills, prepares monthly income statements and balance sheets for Board review and, critically, prepares the annual budget (which determines the amount of members' quarterly dues). He has ALWAYS been responsive and thorough in the performance of those duties.

Bob Hoover, Member-at-Large, put his Information Technology background to work by maintaining the club's laptop computer – used by speakers for their presentations& – and, with the help of his wife, Karen, prepared a Facebook page for the club.

The most challenging activity for the year was attracting and retaining members. 2015 saw the resignation of 10 members but only the acquisition of 2 new members (as well as 2 associate members). Some efforts to address this situation were taken: Wayne Strasbaugh formed a membership committee and John White prepared a new membership brochure to take advantage of our new venue for lunches. But, 2016 will have to be a year of an aggressive drive for expanding our rolls.

Finally, I want to thank George Fisher for producing this annual publication and John White for producing the President's dinner program. These members continue to give the club their time, talent and treasure.

Carter Broach
http://www.philadelphia-reflections.com/blog/3479.htm

Right Angle 2015 Speakers

Note. Jan. Speakers Arranged by others, 2015 program chair not present.

Feb. 6 John Caskey, Ph D *(Philadelphia SD Finances and Governance.)*

Feb. 13 Jeffery La Monica, Ph D *(Chemical Warfare in WWI.)*

Feb. 20 Tony Junker *(Peace Museum for Philadelphia).*

Feb. 27 Joel Spivak *(Subways Around the World.)*

Mar. 13 Bob Fernandez, Inquirer *(Net Neutrality; How, What, Why?)*

Mar. 20 Rodger Lane, Ph D *(History of Crime.)*

Mar. 27 Chad Bardone *(Peace Corps Then and Now.)*

Apr. 10 Krystak Appiah *(Northern African American Experience post Civil War.)*

Apr. 17 Robert Margolskee, Ph D and MD *(How Taste and Smell Relate to Health.)*

Apr. 24 Michael Comfort *(How the Navy Won the Civil War.)*

May. 1 David Specca *(Environmental Agriculture and Bio Energy.)*

May. 8 David Richman Walter Russell, *(Self Bestowed Genius.)*

May. 29 Frank Bell *(The Soga Brothers, Art and; Revenge in Japan.)*

June. 5 Zenos Frudakis *(Philosopher in Clay.)*

June. 12 Stephen Clowery *(Leica and the Birth of 35mm Photography.)*

June. 19 Bruce Mowday *(Pickett's Charge; The Untold Story.)*

June. 26 Berine Enright *(A Fresh Look at George Washington.)*

July. 10 Allan Brink *(Spring City Electrical: An Enduring History.)*

July. 17 Ina Lipman *(The Children's Scholarship Fund.)*

July. 24 Thayer Schroeder *(History of WaWa.)*

July. 31 Jose Benitez *(Needle Exchange in Philadelphia.)*

Aug. 7 George Strimel *(SEPTA in Motion.)*

Aug. 14 Ned Rauch-Mannino *(Marcellus Shale Gas Use Impact on Philadelphia.)*

Aug. 21 Patrica Dickey *(Brazil-Philadelphia Chamber of Commerce.)*

Aug. 28 Jason Mayland *(Charter School Successes and Failures.)*

Sept. 18 Ted Burkett *(Las Pozas: An Eccentric Englishman's Mexican Fantasy.)*

Oct. 2 Eugene DiOrio *(Lukens Steel and Rebecca Lukens.)*

Oct. 9 M. Fredric Riedersd, Ph. D *(Last Chance Crime.)*

Oct. 16 Donna A. Bilak, Ph. D *(The Chymical Cleric: the Remarkable Story of John Allin, Puritan Alchemist.)*

Oct. 23 Jeffery H. Johnson, Ph. D *(From Dyes to Destruction: The German Chemical Industry in WW I.)*

Oct. 31 Mary Anne Eves *(The 1876 Centennial in Philadelphia: America's First World's Fair.)*

Nov. 6 Al Markle *(Vietnam- A Veteran's New Perspective.)*

Nov. 13 Allan Silverberg, et al *(Holocaust Rememberance.)*

Nov. 20 David Hollenberg *(University of Pennsylvania's Architecture.)*

Dec. 11 Dominc Tierney, Ph. D *(The Right Way to Lose a War to Lose a War: America in an Age of Unwinnable Conflicts.)*

Dec. 18 Matt Duppee *(Men's Clubs in Philadelphia and Beyond.)*

http://www.philadelphia-reflections.com/blog/3441.htm

Economic Proposals For 2015-16, A Trial Balloon

Glenn Hubbard, former Chairman of George W. Bush's Council of Economic Advisers, has written his proposals for 2015-2016 as an Op-Ed piece in the *New York Times*, in January, 2015. The choice of newspaper probably has some significance, since the Chairman of a President's Council of Economic advisers sometimes does, and sometimes does not, formulate the economics views of his party and his President. It's possible he seeks to influence the role of his party's Congressional leaders, or possibly represents the views of the two former Bush Presidents, or even a variant of them meant to influence Jeb Bush in his run for the 2017 Presidency. Time will probably tell, as the last two years of the Obama second term could be a time of compromise, or a time of bitter dissention. Hubbard makes ten or eleven points, usually as single-sentence assertions without associated arguments.

Broadened Budget Neutrality. The first point is that Congress has long been working within the boundaries of tax neutrality for any changes in the tax revenue derived from individual social or economic classes, a restriction Hubbard feels is unnecessary. The example he gives is corporate income taxation, which is very likely the area he had in mind. Perhaps, I think he is suggesting, corporate taxes could usefully be lowered without considering the personal benefits to the upper class of corporation stockholders. In effect, Labor Unions are seen to be acting out the attitudes of the Molly Maguire's, in which only cigar-smoking plutocrats would be gaining if the corporations they own were taxed less. In the Gilded Age, perhaps family-owned corporations were the norm, but for fifty years American corporations (but strangely, not German corporations) have been stockholder-owned, or even index-fund owned. And if not officially, individual retirement assets are a growing part of every family's savings. There was a time when only rich folk owned stock, but nowadays employee pension assets have become a growing power in the marketplace. Double taxation is much less a class issue than formerly, and perhaps even cigar-smoking union bosses can be persuaded to change their stance and their rhetoric. Lowering corporate taxes might well help the working class more than the top one percent of earners if matters were scored in a balanced way.

Flattening the Steep Step A second point is made that increasing subsidies and tax credits for the poor, leads to a steep step up to employment and a sudden loss of subsidies, as a further hindrance to joining the work force. Deriding the loss of subsidies as favoring the "trickle down" process, is an unfortunate obstacle to searching for more gradual approaches to general prosperity.

Consolidated Business Tax. An effort to achieve a gradual transition is suggested, of a consolidated business tax rather than industry taxes and exemptions, and very likely a gradual merger of the customary bank loans, versus bonds. There is a sound of general plausibility about this, but no reasoning is offered in the editorial. Depreciation might be loosened somewhat for the general purpose of increased flexibility, but in general the main area where depreciation ought to be made merely discretionary, is in non-profit companies.

Specifying the Top Tax Bracket. It's interesting to read Mr. Hubbard's proposal to make the top bracket for personal income tax the same as the top bracket for business income. The reasoning behind this proposal is not given, and is not immediately obvious. However, it does seem to be an improvement to have this issue removed from class warfare language of "fairness", to be replaced by some other benchmark with a rationale. Hubbard similarly is inclined to replace subsidies to the poor with tax credits, a move which has the additional advantage of smoothing out the "steep step" up to income tax which is more graduated by effectively having more gradations than merely poverty versus no-poverty. Whether this is the underlying reasoning or not, anything which softens the Molly Maguire rhetoric of the 19th Century coal mines, would be a step forward.

Health Care It certainly is heartening to see Health Savings Accounts recommended in both of the two alternatives he proposes for paying for healthcare, one with continued employer-based insurance and one with a tax deduction on the personal income tax. And it is certainly time for a way to be found to give equal tax deductions to those who pay for their own health insurance.

Educational Tax Deduction. A truly innovative proposal is made about tax deductions. Mr. Hubbard proposes a personal tax deduction for education and training, similar to the one already given for investment in technology and equipment. There's a question of whether this should be given to the individual or his employer, but that can be worked out in Congress. The idea is excellent, particularly when it is limited to out-of-pocket investments in education, since it has the additional potential to address rising tuition costs, while encouraging more education.

Block Grants. It is also innovative to consider block grants to the states to replace the tradition of making Federal funds conditional on state "cooperation", which the Supreme Court has begun to disapprove, as an invasion of states rights. This one might even rise to the level of a proposed Constitutional Amendment. There is little doubt the state legislatures are the weakest part of our federalized system, that the Supreme Court recognizes that fact, and leans toward attributing this problem to the system of conditional grants.

Consolidated Entitlements. Unless I am mistaken, there is a welcome proposal to address entitlement programs by consolidating them; and in the process begin to meet the looming issue of underfunded retirement costs. In a sense, the retirement costs are an outgrowth of improved health and longevity, a truly difficult problem created by a desirable effort.

Let's plan to review this program before the end of the year. By that time, it will have been tested in the fire of adversary process. And since the following year will be disordered by election campaigns, we can then surmise how much will be passed into legislation, how much will be exposed as impractical, and how much will fail passage but become the lore of long-term party positions in the far future.

http://www.philadelphia-reflections.com/blog/2781.htm

2015 As Predicted from Pittsburgh

For the past 14 years, LaSalle University has featured an economics meeting at the Union League in January, usually with an economist predicting the local outlook for the year. Increasingly, the luncheon in Lincoln Hall has been packed, and sponsored by some local firm. This year, the speaker was Stuart A. Hoffman, the chief

Stuart A. Hoffman

Oil

economist of PNC Bank, who turns out to be quite a witty fellow. The lunch itself was gourmet, although a little on the feminine side for a mostly male audience. And because the place was filled with audience, the waitresses of the League were taking it away faster than the eaters could eat it. It's hard to say what the audience might have felt about that, because most of them could afford to lose a few pounds, just like the Chef himself.

Dr. Hoffman feels the big news this year is OIL. It sort of fell out of heaven at the right moment, but even the politicians who opposed it are forced to acknowledge it was a very good thing, indeed. Its international effect, in creating oil independence, was especially powerful and undeniable. However, there are winners and losers. Our North American neighbors in Canada and Mexico may feel some painful effects, for example. In any event, the discovery and exploitation of fracking seems very likely to bring the recession to an end, sooner than we deserve, at least.

So the prediction for the year is rather bright for wages, unemployment, and housing, perhaps even banking. The relevant parts of the stock and bond market will prosper – undeservedly, as always. But at the end of the year, we are likely to see that recovery as historical only, as we begin to see the long term gloom inherent in health care and educational costs, and the rest of the world begins to affect us more than we affect them. How's that for a January prediction, largely revolving around unexpected events in OIL. We'll try to remember to compare this January prediction with the subsequent December retrospective realities, later in this volume. We'll even see if Dr. Hoffman has to eat his words, since today he had very little time to eat his lunch.

In the Question period, it was particularly interesting to hear a short description of what recently happened to the Swiss franc. The Swiss never joined the monetary union, but they did peg their currency to the Euro. As time went on, it was increasingly painful for Swiss exporters to have the franc suppressed by the lagging Euro, and when the Chairman of the European Bank announced his intention to start buying bonds, the Swiss bank capitulated and cut the tie of the Swiss franc to the Euro. The franc promptly

Mario Draghi Chairman of the European Bank

rose, and that's all there is to the matter. Except if it isn't. The Germans are in much the same position within the Euro zone, and the English are restless, outside of it. So, if the prosperous parts of Europe decide to follow the Swiss example, the whole European monetary scheme

Andy Mellon

may be in trouble. And if Europe has a monetary convulsion, its trading partners in Africa and South America may follow, dragging in China, and – who would be so brave as to suggest the USA could remain unaffected? Especially if Putin and the Arabs misbehave, pulverizing Israel in the process. When all you have is a hammer, you treat everything as a nail. Central Asia used to have two things, oil and ruffians. And now they have apparently lost their dominance in oil.

Well, that's about the size of it, from Pittsburgh. Pittsburgh was largely settled by going West on the Erie Canal, so they never liked being attached to the Quaker end of the state. Philadelphia dominated with its banks, to Andy Mellon's great distaste, and largely controlled the shift of steel production from Eastern anthracite to Western bituminous coal. So now, Philadelphia scarcely has a bank to its name, and has to hear the News of the World in Review – from the other end of the state.

http://www.philadelphia-reflections.com/blog/2777.htm

Two Chapters of the World Economy's History

World Economic History, Chapter One.

In 1972 Richard Nixon and Henry Kissinger persuaded China to change sides. As a consequence, America and the Far East prospered, Soviet Russia collapsed, Europe devoted its attention to a twenty-hour week. The American consumer had a picnic at bargain prices, but it was too much of a leap for the Chinese consumer, so the party leaders prospered mightily from corruption, nepotism and casino gambling.

After America then over-invested in affordable housing, and Wall Street distributed the profits through the securities markets, their stock markets froze in a panic, then collapsed. The American government rescued Bear Stearns, but then reversed itself and refused to bail out Lehman Brothers. Its markets collapsed further, its economy ground to a halt, and the Federal Reserve lowered long-term interest rates with Quantitative Easing, while Congress imposed the Dodd-Frank financial regulation bill.

The economy responded with a very slow recovery from the crash, and in seven years was still not fully recovered, except Quantitative Easing maintained abnormally low interest rates, so the American consumer went on a spending spree.

World Economic History, Chapter Two.

By 2015, the Chinese consumer was getting restless because of failure to participate in the boom, so the Chinese premier clamped down on leadership corruption, plus devaluing its currency.

The Chinese leadership, who owned most of the stock, responded to what seemed like an attack on its privileges, by dumping its stock holdings; the Chinese market crashed, followed by the rest of the world to a lesser degree. The Federal Reserve had promised to raise interest rates, but became fearful of making the crash worse.

The American stockholder had been told this was what had happened in the crash of 1937, which had been worse for the stockholder than 1929. Others said it was mostly a Chinese problem. The Federal Reserve continued to hold $3 trillion of Treasury bonds. During all this Keynesian activity, American inflation remained below its 2% target, at 1.5%, some say actually 0.3%. Manipulation of our currency or markets was suspected, a practically unheard-of event in view of our size.

So, what seems to have happened is the collapse of the Chinese stockmarket scared the wits out of the American stockmarket, which dropped like a stone. And that seems to have frightened the Federal Reserve into saying it wasn't so sure it wanted to raise interest rates, after all. So the American stockmarket shot up like a rocket, recovering most of its losses. It may be a happy result, but how many times can we repeat it?

And then, the Developing countries, which sell raw materials to China, dropped. And then Europe announced it was going to do Quantitative Easing, because – horrors – there hadn't been the inflation they hoped for. Which reminded everyone that Obama had spent more money than Congress appropriated, forcing US to borrow more, or else shut the government down. The flood of Treasury bonds seems to be what holds down inflation, since the market responds to a flood of bonds by lowering interest rates. Perhaps we do not need a debt limit, if the market imposes its will, placing a limit on borrowing. The American stock market is on the way down, unless Obama stops borrowing, or until Congress raises taxes. And, curiously, it seems to be China that gets hurt, first.

http://www.philadelphia-reflections.com/blog/3370.htm

The Streets of Philadelphia, on Ben Franklin's Birthday

Benjamin Franklin
309th Birthday

They changed the calendar in the Eighteenth Century, so it's always confusing to talk about the birthdays of the Founding Fathers. Benjamin Franklin for example was born on January 6, 1705, but by the time he got around to being famous, he was born on January 17, 1706. Scholars handle this awkwardness by saying he was born on January 17, 1706 [OS, January 6, 1705]. That's not all the problem, however. This year on January 17 he had his 309th birthday, unless you wish to say he had his 310th birthday on January 6. The novelty has long since worn off, and nowadays most birthday celebrants prefer just not to mention the matter. You might think Don Smith would think this is of vital importance, but he cheerfully brushes it off with a chuckle.

Ben Franklin Celebration

Don Smith is the current ringleader of the Ben Franklin Birthday Celebration, which is held at 9 AM every year, on January 17th [NS], starting at the American Philosophical Society's Franklin Hall on Chestnut Street, once a very substantially-built bank building. The constituent members are affiliated with one of the thirty-odd organizations which Franklin founded, although anyone interested is welcomed. On what usually turns out to be the coldest day of the year, the birthday celebrants gather for hot drinks and cookies, followed by one or two really outstanding lectures about Franklin. Sometimes the lecture's connection to Franklin is a little stretched, but all of them are excellent. At 11 AM, the group marches together to Ben's grave at 5th and Arch for a short ceremony, led by Franklin reinactors and honest-to-goodness members in the uniform of the National Guard, which Franklin founded. He did so when the Spanish and French ships were bombarding the coast, and as the editor of the town's newspaper, Franklin called for troops to defend us.

Paul R. Levy

The Quaker government declined to be violent, so Franklin published an invitation for volunteers to bring their guns and join him. Ten thousand showed up, and Franklin's career in public life was established. He was a hero to everyone – except Thomas Penn, who saw him as a threat. Much subsequent Colonial history revolves around this episode and its consequences.

After the march, the group settles down for a good lunch, and hears yet another outstanding lecture. This year it was given by Stephen Levy, the President of a planning organization called the Center City District. Steve's message this year was about how the streets of Center City Philadelphia were constructed for walking, or at most riding horseback. That is, they were narrow. They widened somewhat as they went West and had to accommodate a city of carriages. That was quite good enough through the Gilded Age, when Philadelphia could credibly claim to be the richest city in the world.

Automobile

But then what happened was not the two World Wars, the stock market crash of 1929, or anything resembling that. What happened in Steve Levy's view, was the automobile. Hundreds, then thousands of autos filled the streets, scattering chickens and children, and eventually making the city impassible. Nothing would do but to move to the suburbs, which among other things provided the thrill of driving too fast and too carelessly, and reducing the pedestrians while increasing the business of accident rooms. There was certainly no room for bicycles, which were driven away without a tear being shed, and defying the efforts of city planners to find a safe place for them. Europe, good old Europe where we came from, was more successful in hounding the imposter autos off the bike paths of Amsterdam and Copenhagen. And preserving intercity high speed train service, at great taxpayer expense. Those Europeans really know how to live, in sidewalk cafes, unaffected by bicycles, preserving a much older collection of narrow city streets leading to empty cathedrals, in Germany, France, and Central Europe. That wasn't the American way, at all. We just pulled up sticks and moved to the suburbs, abandoning the dirty old defeated cities to their ethnic neighborhoods.

It's a novel theory, and maybe even a correct one. It could explain a lot, if Philadelphia is seen as a victim of Detroit, strangling on their mutual industrial excesses.

http://www.philadelphia-reflections.com/blog/2778.htm

Suburb in the Big City

In gathering views on what made Philadelphia deteriorate, a rather surprising response was given by Don Roberts, of Brown Brothers, Harriman. Don had obviously given this matter considerable thought, and without a moment's hesitation he answered, "The City-County Consolidation of 1858." For a few weeks, I puzzled over this answer, but my older daughter Miriam suddenly made it clear.

Miriam lives in Chestnut Hill, the suburb within the city. Her answer was made up of two anecdotes, relating personal experiences with city employees. The first had to do with the Water Department, which I had always heard was the crown jewel of the City bureaucracy. One day, she had no water in her house. Her first impulse, for whatever reason, was to call Roto Router. The nice man came and told her her pipes were fine, but the water had been turned off at the street, and he was forbidden to turn it back on. Happens all the time, he said, and he knew it was a waste of time to call anyone but the City. After several phone calls to the Water Department, the department sent out a man. At first, the Water Department denied they had turned it off. The next day a man came and, well, Yes, we did turn it off. Your next door neighbor hadn't paid her water bill, so we sent a man to turn off her water. He couldn't find her pipe, so he turned off the nearest thing he could find, which happened to be yours. After hearing my daughter screech in her best accent, they turned it back on. Sorry about that.

The second anti-city-consolidation episode was to discover a uniformed city employee rummaging in her garbage. Asked what he was doing, he announced he was fining her $85 for failing to separate garbage from trash. After being told she was freakishly diligent in doing so, and was in fact one of the founding members of Earth Day, he rummaged some more and found a cardboard box with some strawberry juice smeared on it. So, she took the next day off from work, went down to headquarters to spend the whole day, and had the satisfaction of having the fine removed. Her neighbors later told her, happens all the time. When it happens to them, they just pay the fine and shrug it off.

Those of us who live in the unconsolidated suburbs are universally of the opinion that neither of these episodes could possibly have ever happened in their suburb, because suburban officials listen to the citizens. Come to think of it, I'll plan to ask Don Roberts where he lives, just to see if this was the point he was making.

http://www.philadelphia-reflections.com/blog/2782.htm

River to River, Pine to Vine

Brad Mills, a former Marine officer who now is a Commercial real estate advisor for Tactix Real Estate Advisors, was recently on the podium of the Right Angle Club. His theme was the Decline of the Suburbs, creating a return to Center City. Although some other cities have experienced an even greater change, his point generally corresponds to everyone's experience. If Stephen Levy is right that the automobile choked center city to death in the 1920s, this reversal of fortunes would seem to correct the migration of a century ago. The big question is whether it will continue, once an economic recovery, and cheap gasoline prices, make the auto popular again.

The Center City scene at present is summarized by its rental prices: $100 per square foot for offices, $400 per square foot for top-level residential. So, naturally there are a number of office buildings being transformed into either residential or mixed-use. And about 20% of office space is unoccupied. The offices themselves are being transformed into a style which absolutely no one likes. Open space offices with insignificant partitions between them. Even the top officers are forced to abandon corner offices in order to show the rest of the employees they are participating in the new style, which as mentioned, everyone hates. Another statistic: the office space averages ten units per 1000 square feet, instead of the more luxurious 4 per thousand, and more often single offices. SEI carries matters to some sort of extreme: desks on wheels can be gathered together for conferences, pulled apart to talk on the phone. And to make things even worse, this seems to be following a European style. Ugh. For one thing, no American likes to appear European. No one likes it when office space is "hotelized", sharing a desk between someone in the office and someone else who is on the road, visiting the trade.

There's a lot of talk of Drexel showing us the future, but that's probably in the far future, when Drexel has to consider building over the West Philadelphia train tracks along the river, for dormitories or whatever. In time that may happen, but what's immediately in prospect is the second building Comcast is building next to the existing one. To a degree, the people who will fill the new building are already here, scattered out in vacant spaces around City Hall. When the building is finished, those people will move into it, leaving their existing space – either empty, if the recession continues, or occupied with "secondary" offices if we recover from the recession in time. It's a time of anxiety for architects.

And the people? Well, we have a doughnut hole model. The top executives want to be in town, close to work, where the action is. And young couples want to save on commuting expenses, living close to work, using public transport, living close to other people their own age. Out in the suburbs, things are emptying out, prices are down, and "crazy money" from New York is moving in for what they imagine are bargains. It promises to be an exciting scene, full of action. But what's missing? School age children. It won't be much of a normal city without some kids, and to get them you need good schools, public safety, and a shift in taxes from that 19th Century wage tax, to the more modern real estate tax. Meanwhile, our speaker has his own individual office – in Radnor.

http://www.philadelphia-reflections.com/blog/2783.htm

Gashouse Gang

A couple of lawyers from Community Legal Services dropped around to the Franklin Inn club, the other day. Someone in the club thought they might be able to shed some light on the recent sale, or rather frustrated sale, of the Philadelphia Gas Works and invited them over. They told us what they knew, but other luncheon guests came away with the impression they don't know the full scoop. It's for sure the newspapers don't know much, either.

Philadelphia's Gas Company was started in 1830, and acquired as a City property in 1860. Before that time, an occasional mansion would have its own private gas house, fermenting gas for central lighting and heating, and apparently the scene of other carryings-on, leading to the derogatory title of "Gas House Gang". That was long before any thought of city corruption, or politics, or even professional Baseball. For nearly a century, municipal gas works would produce "Manufacturer's Gas" by fermentation of various discarded materials, but when the "Big Inch" pipeline was converted to natural gas at the end of the World War II, at least people stopped committing suicide with it (natural gas didn't work), and most cities sold the gas company to private owners. Gas work have long had the reputation of featherbedding and corruption, selective collection of gas bills, and a fair amount of graft. Perhaps much of this is a legend of the past, but I wouldn't bet much money on it. It suddenly got into the news lately, when a Connecticut company made a cash offer for PGW, the local gas company. The Mayor liked the idea and brought it to City Council, which refused even to consider it. The newspapers had recently had a run-in with Mr. Dougherty, the President of the Electricians Union, over the conviction of the union for arson of the Chestnut Hill Quaker Meeting House, and there's no doubt the news coverage of the Gashouse sale offered the public a dim perception of City Council politicians and their pro-union behavior.

Our lawyer guests felt this was a little unfair. The Mayor did request a hearing on the matter, but he is not a member of City Council, and needed a member to introduce the topic for discussion. After the Council President expressed an unfavorable position, no other member of Council was willing to introduce it. So the matter was dropped for lack of a sponsor. While there is little doubt much was beneath the surface, it is a little imprecise to say the Council blocked the matter from consideration. The next time the City Charter comes up for review, it would seem reasonable to allow the Mayor to introduce measures by himself, perhaps by giving him ex officio membership. Leaving him without some way to start a discussion, as he was humiliated to admit in public, does seem a little awkward. But it permits it to be said they actively blocked him, in this particular case.

Let's be sure we remember the biggest news in this state for a decade, has been the discovery of shale gas, leading to energy independence, low energy prices, and potential prosperity. Governor Corbett had refused to allow taxes on the shale extraction, and a lot of politicians had been counting on getting a piece of this action for their own local purposes. In the November 2014 election, there had been a Republican landslide across the whole nation, including the Pennsylvania Legislature. But Republican Governor Corbett was swept out of office, in a striking exception to the landslide. One of the visiting lawyers mused that Philadelphia's Democratic Mayor was probably looking for some state assistance in his struggling budget problems, and perhaps, just perhaps, that was the reason he was acting in such a wayward manner in this gashouse thing. No one was talking. After all, it was common belief that gas transmission lines were all sewed up, many stronger politicians had got there first, and gas for Philadelphia was a non-starter. Since no one is willing to talk about it, everybody has a right to his own guess. Here's mine.

A thing is worth what you can sell it for, not a penny more. The President of a Connecticut gas company presumably has something on his mind when he crosses two state lines to make an offer for some distant city's gas company. Two possibilities come to mind immediately, and one of them is immediately squelched. That would have been the idea that the acquiring company would plan to dump the defined-benefit pension plan of the city employees, and offer a defined-contribution plan like everyone else. But that idea had occurred to others first, and it had been testified the pension plan for the gas workers was actually pretty well funded. So, if that's a non-starter, there's only one other excuse the Connecticut gas president could offer to his own Board of Directors, for pursuing a $42 million cost to acquire a $30 million dollar savings, particularly when PGW already had the highest rates in the state and obviously wouldn't be able to raise them after a merger.

It would be my guess this talk about the hopelessness of getting a pipe line constructed, was bunkum. My suspicion is he had good reason to believe he could get a pipeline, and that a Republican president would approve it. Governor Corbett had already shown unusual foresight in attracting pipelines by refusing to tax shale gas. By the time he got the pipe in the ground, a gas glut would drop gas prices so severely no competitor in another state could compete with it. That's why the dimwits in the Legislature were so mad at him; they were expecting a joy ride on those taxes for themselves. Instead, we have taken a couple of steps toward making Pennsylvania the oil capital of a nation which has shale competition in forty other states. But Pennsylvania would have the pipelines. Poor Corbett got a political pistol-whipping, but if he has friends who owe him bigtime in the oil business, he won't be permanently sorry.

http://www.philadelphia-reflections.com/blog/2794.htm

Philadelphia School Crisis

John Caskey, a professor at Swarthmore, recently visited the Right Angle Club to share his insights into the origins and potential solutions to the approaching collapse of the Philadelphia School system. The problem, everyone agrees, seems even more devastating in the light of the eminence of the Philadelphia schools, public and private, until very recently. While the elephant in the parlor is the 1940's migration of poor black people from the Southern states to the northern ones, it does seem to be true that the very eminence of the Catholic School system, and the Quaker private school system, has served to aggravate rather than rescue the situation. For example, when parochial schools are forced to close, there is no pool of tax money to transfer with them to charter schools. Philadelphia had been able to afford better public schools while the private schools supported themselves. But when their support diminished, their closure did not unleash any funds to help the public system. By contrast, when a public school closes, the tax money is transferred to the charter schools. One third of all children entering Philadelphia charter schools, are coming from parochial schools. It would be interesting to learn whether the total school budget, public and private together, had actually been less than it is today.

Without access to the specific facts, it would seem likely the number of children attending Philadelphia schools must have shrunk considerably in the past few decades. You can close or even sell, empty school houses, but pensions reflect the number of teachers when the city population was larger. Something like that seems plausible as an explanation for Philadelphia teachers receiving an average of $70,000 apiece, while at the same time, reliable figures seems to show an average per teacher employment cost of $110,000. Possibly true, but probably misleading. Almost everyone acknowledges we cannot afford the municipal pension system of the Great Depression of the 1930s, but it is almost too late to do much about those costs, magnified as they must be, by having a disproportionate amount of the school budget go to retirees.

The social intractability of the problem is brought out by some comparisons of the source of school revenue. Because Philadelphia is poor, while the suburbs are comparatively affluent, one would expect the suburbs to have a greater proportion of their school budgets derived from local property taxes. Actually, matters are exactly the reverse. Poor as it is, Philadelphia is supporting over 80% of school costs from local taxes, while the suburbs are much more supported by state and federal sources. The failing city school system is in fact draining the limited local real estate taxes away from other expenditures which might restore some of its affluence. And it isn't likely to restore the balance, any time soon. Real estate specialists refer to the "donut hole", by which they mean that parents of school-age children move away to better and safer schools. As soon as things improve somewhat, we can expect school children to flood back into town, bringing their expenses with them. We have yielded to expedients which in a sense represented our financial reserves. We must overcome this obstacle before much progress is even possible.

Even our political correct speech gets in the road of progress. There is a notable reluctance to blame the school problem on the migration of poor black people from the rural areas of the South, to the inner cities of the North. But it is plainly true; our resources have been overwhelmed by this phenomenon of the 1940s. Air conditioning did improve the livability of the South, drawing Northern industries Southward. Since this aspect of the issue is an interstate problem, federalism hampers the efforts to send tax money Northwards to balance things. We mustn't talk about things like that, right? To some considerable degree, this problem resembles the international balance of trade. When trade migrates in one direction, funds must migrate in the opposite direction. To whatever degree our fastidiousness of speech hampers this self-balancing, it makes the problem worse.

http://www.philadelphia-reflections.com/blog/2795.htm

Tony Junker; Peace Museum

The Right Angle Club was once again honored by a recent talk by Tony Junker, the novelist, retired architect, center City resident – and now the leader in an effort to start a Peace Museum. He's a Quaker, as Philadelphians would easily guess, and a charming peace advocate. He tells us his specialty while a practicing architect, was designing museums, so the whole thing starts to fit together. The museum is still in the planning stages, hoping to raise two million dollars

Tony Junker

as start-up money. Needless to say, Philadelphia has a long history of Quaker advocacy for Peace. It is not saying too much to suppose William Penn designed his whole colony as a peace demonstration. And Tony began his talk by noting that in England, Penn's father remains much better known than his son.

William senior conquered the island of Jamaica and gave it to King Charles, in return for which the King repaid his debt by giving the admiral's son Pennsylvania. On his deathbed, the Admiral beseeched his king to look after his rebellious and somewhat disobedient son; this was King Charles' way of doing it. By the way, he had distinguished himself with successful administration of New Jersey before the King gave him Pennsylvania, and acquired what is now the state of Delaware, somewhat later. With these three states, he became the largest private landowner in our history – ever. He makes the Klebergs of the

King Ranch look pretty paltry by comparison, and indeed Charles even offered to make him a vassal king. Young William, however, told him that really wasn't the idea, at all. Young

The Peace Museum

Penn sold land to his suspicious co-religionists, and in order to facilitate the sales, drew up a document called, <u>Concessions and Agreements</u>, which was in considerable part a model for America's Constitution. It can be found in the Archives of the State of New Jersey, in Trenton.

The Peace Museum is projected to open in a few years; it would be a great mistake to underestimate Tony's ability to get it started. Since his retirement, he has founded a Quaker retirement community on Front Street which is already in existence. It's open to non-Quakers of course, and there are quite a few Quaker retirement villages in the suburbs. But Philadelphia is returning to Center City, and the need for a retirement home has often been expressed, but never implemented until Tony came along. Early Quakers lived in caves along the banks of the Delaware River, just about where the retirement village is situated, and Quaker settlement later concentrated along Arch Street. Arch Street, by the way, really had an arch. Evidently, the river was once much deeper and

somewhat wider, so it had one embankment which began at Front Street, and a lower one on Water Street. So as the town grew, it was natural to undercut a tunnel with an arch bearing Front Street. Many houses eventually had one door on Water Street and another door on Front Street, higher up. Relics of Quaker settlement can still be noticed on Arch Street, cut off by the Benjamin Franklin Parkway slanting Northward. Front and Arch was the location for the main anchorage in those days, and the London Tavern at Front and

Whiskey Rebellion

Market was the main hangout of sailors off the ships nearby, a rich source of gossip and the origin of a number of rebellious episodes. The Fifteenth Street Meetinghouse now seems to be the most westward sign of this Quaker settlement, but Isaac Sharpless bought the Land of Friends Select School further west, and shared the land between Friends Select and his high-rise headquarters of what was the Pennwalt headquarters. If you are planning a Quaker museum in Center City, you can find plenty of choices to be called historic Quaker property, along Arch Street. The still earlier Quaker settlements around Dock Creek, beginning at about Spruce Street, have long been outgrown and abandoned.

Unfortunately, although we experienced long periods of Peace during the Nineteenth Century, it must be admitted that Penn's hope for an example of peaceful existence to the rest of the world, would have to be called a failure. We have had several major foreign wars during the Twenty-first century, and show every sign of preparing for more. The Quakers literally owned a major portion of the American colonies, and withdrew from politics rather than vote for war taxes in the Revolutionary War. While the example of courageous conscientious objection had its impact, it also developed an image of martyrdom which the rest of the world declines to imitate. Friends are perfectly capable of forming their own opinions, but it might be suggested to them that more of their efforts would be successful if somehow they made more publicity of their successes.

George Washington, for example, was effective in keeping us out of foreign entanglement, in large part by the fact that he was a famous athlete, and a successful warrior. His example for the country was in effect, "If you are strong, people leave you alone." He was surely successful in achieving a peaceful settlement of the Whiskey Rebellion by saddling up his horse and riding at the head of 10,000 troops in a threatening manner. Later in his presidential administration he was surely more effective in dealing with European powers because of his former military reputation, than he would have been without it. His second inaugural address was in effect a plea that good things could emerge from self-interest: Honesty is the best policy. There's a primitive quality to this appeal, reminding his countrymen they are more likely to get rich if they were honest, than if they were dishonest. Purists may squirm at the undertones of this motto, but surely it was effective with his countrymen. And three quarters of the world's population might still be better off if they adopted a motto which falls just a little short of being altruistic.

http://www.philadelphia-reflections.com/blog/2813.htm

Paying for the Healthcare of Children

It has been said by others that eventually healthcare will shrink down to paying for the first year of life, and the last one. Right up to that final moment, medical payments must somehow evolve in two opposite directions. We might just as well imagine two complimentary payment systems immediately, because the two persisting methodologies could eventually conflict unless planned for. Paying in advance is fundamentally cheaper than paying after the service is rendered, because there is no potential for default in payment.

The two methods even result in different aggregate prices; in one case you pay to borrow, while in the other you get paid to loan the money. Dual systems are a fair amount of trouble; remember how long it took gasoline filling stations to adjust to credit cards versus cash. When gas prices eventually got high enough, they just charged everybody a single price, again. This isn't just lower middle-class stubbornness. Dual payment systems slow you down, and profit is generated from repeated rapid transactions. The buyer wants the goods and the seller wants the money. Profit comes from doing exchanges as fast and often as you can manage them.

In a well-designed lifetime scheme, with balances successively transferred from one pidgeon-hole to another, it becomes possible to maintain a positive balance for years at a time (thereby reducing final prices, because the income from compound interest keeps rising toward its far end). That was a discovery of the ancient Greeks, but sometimes Benjamin Franklin seems like the only person to have noticed.

However, in real-life health costs, there is one intractable exception. Because obstetrics can be costly, particularly the high costs of prematurity and congenital abnormalities, the first year of life averages $10,500, or 3% of present total health costs. It therefore results in pricing which many young

> *"The last year of life is more expensive,*
> *But the first year of life may cause more financial pain."*

parents cannot afford, in spite of insurance overcharges to catch up later. And thereby a multi-year stretch of interest income is jumbled up, often lost entirely. It gets worse: childhood costs from birth to age 21 average 8% of lifetime healthcare. Please notice: Single-year term insurance premiums always rise to a much higher level than lifetime, or whole-life, premium costs, because internal float compounds in whole-life. Modern medicine has also resulted in rising lifetime costs, with only this obstetrical exception. Someone surely would have figured this out, except excessive taxation of corporations created a motive not to notice the effect on tax exempted expenditures.

This problem obviously could be approached by borrowing or subsidizing. Someone might even envision a complicated process of transferring obstetrical costs to the grandparents for thirty-five years, then transferring the costs back to the parent generation. Since we are describing a cradle-to-grave scheme, it seems much better to imagine a single person's costs eventually becoming unified. Grandparents do in fact share continuous protoplasm with grandchildren, but before that was recognized, the courts had decided a new life begins when a baby's ears reach the sunlight. *Stare decisis* beats biology, almost every time. A society which already has a high divorce rate and a great deal of other family upheaval, probably feels better suited to the principle of "Every ship on its own bottom." – except for this financing issue. For childless couples and parentless children, some kind of pooling is possibly more appealing, and the complexities of modern life may eventually lead that way.

In the meantime, lawyers, who see a great deal of human weakness, are probably better suited to suggest a methodology for transferring average birth costs between generations, and back, although a voluntary process seems more flexible. It would seem grandparents are often most likely to be in a position to leave a few thousand dollars to grandchildren in their wills, and age thirty-five to forty seems the time when competing costs are at a lifetime low, making that the best time to pay it back.

Some grandparents are destitute however, and some parents are basketball stars. There are surely generalizations with many exceptions. The process is happily simplified by a birth rate of 2.1 children per couple, which is also 1:1 at the grandparent/grandchild level, and our Society has an unspoken wish to increase the birth rate if it could afford it. For legal default purposes, matrilineal rather than patrilineal descent may be more workable. But – if every grandparent willed an appropriate amount to some grandchild's account, it would work out (with a small balancing pool), creating a small incentive for the intermediate generation to have more children.

The answer to this dilemma probably lies in revising the estate-resolution process, making HSA-to-HSA transfers largely automatic within families, devising a common law of special exceptions and adjustments, and creating a pooling system for special cases which defy simple-minded equity. A large proportion of grandparents have an indisputable defined obligation, and a large proportion of grandchildren have an indisputable entitlement. The difficult problems reside in the exceptions, and require a Court of Equity to decide them. We leave it to others to fill in the details, because there could be many ways to accomplish this, and some people have strong preferences. The basics of this situation are the grandparents with surplus funds are likely to die later, but they are still likely to die, close to the age when newborns are appearing on the scene.

When you get down to it, the problem isn't hard if you want to solve it. By arranging lifetime deposits in advance, a large number of grandparents could die with an HSA surplus of appropriate size. A large number of children will be born without a standard-issue family and need the money. After the standard-issue cases have been automatically settled, these outliers can be referred to a Court of Equity charged with doing their best. After a few years of this, the results can be referred back to a Committee of Congress to revise the rules.

A basic fact stands out: most newborn children create a healthcare deficit averaging 8% of $350,000, or $29,000, by the time they reach age 21. Most young parents have difficulty funding so much, and so all lifetime schemes face failure unless something unconventional is done to help it. A dozen more or less legitimate objections can be imagined, but seem worth sacrificing to make lifetime healthcare supportable. The main alternative is to pour enormous sums into the government pool, and then redistribute them. I am uneasy about letting government get deeply mixed into something so personal. So, speaking as a great-grandfather myself, about all that leaves as a potential source of funds, is grandpa, and even grandpas sometimes have an aversion to long hair and rock music.

http://www.philadelphia-reflections.com/blog/2811.htm

"Scores of Centimillionaires"

John Bogle is an investor with an evangelistic twist. He sold over 800,000 copies of his various books about Mutual Funds, donating the royalties to charity. One theme running throughout his writing is that no unmargined investment manager can focus exclusively on equities in his portfolio and expect to have a higher return than the index itself, whether he is an index investor, or is more activist as a portfolio manager. About five or ten percent of managers do beat the index each year, but they are generally managers of small funds, and generally cannot repeat the performance consistently. It's a very useful message, since the conclusion seems to follow that if a manager simply imitates the index, he will surely reduce his research costs, and will therefore almost surely have consistent final results which beat the average competitor. Ultimately, the best results will be found in long-term index funds with the lowest costs. That's a conclusion both logical and borne out by results; no amount of denial can refute the logic of it.

However, it is also possible to take it as a challenge. What approaches might be tested, to see if they can beat it? Mr. Bogle himself admits success might defeat a front-runner, by attracting so many investors the portfolio is forced to limit itself to large-size, when the supply of frisky small stocks gets used up. If the small newcomers out-perform the blue chips, average big-fund performance will suffer by comparison with small boutique funds. Indeed, small-fund indices often display a 2% outperformance, compared with large-cap indices. It would probably be useful to consider closing a large fund to new purchases, when the average size of its investment is forced to contract downward. Since such a reaction benefits the investors but not the managers, the right to close or reopen funds should be transferred to the shareholder investors.

New Tools. It is common for mutual funds to limit or forbid short-selling, as well as buying on margin. That's obviously less risky than engaging in such activity, but most investors understand greater returns require greater risk. That seems to be the approach adopted by hedge funds, although the success of it is often shrouded in secrecy for good reason, and has nothing in common with other stockmarket talents like demanding high fees. The main limitation on hedge fund competition comes from the excessive fees (2% annually, regardless of profits, plus 20% of profits themselves, and a five-year lock-in.) In effect, such activities can be simulated by funds controlled by a single university or pension fund. A fund with a large float of incoming deposits can treat the float as a virtual loan, and an organization which needs to mortgage a large construction project can treat the construction loan on the building as a virtual mortgage on the stock portfolio. It might further be argued that other organizations without a stock portfolio are overweighted in fixed assets whenever they take out a mortgage. Closed-end investment trusts seldom leverage overtly, but they usually are sold at a 10-20% discount to net asset value, and thus are effectively leveraged. Warren Buffett, the greatest stockmarket manager in history, owes much of his success to buying an auto insurance company outright, and then using its float from premium deposits as if they were part of his portfolio. He tends to buy entire companies; their dividends disappear. In special circumstances with 1% prevailing interest rates, it can be difficult to make the case that borrowing is too risky for long-term investments; the issue now is liquidity.

And one final warning. When too many people get overleveraged, by whatever method, they generally sense the approaching dangers, but often are restrained from selling by the tax consequences they would experience. But when it looks as though everybody sees the same thing, there may be a rush for the door. It's called a crash. So don't you dare buy on margin. Let me do it, and together we'll blame the speculators.

REFERENCES

Common Sense on Mutual Funds: Fully Updated 10th Anniversary Edition: John C. Bogle ISBN: 978-0-470138137	Amazon

http://www.philadelphia-reflections.com/blog/2815.htm

New Looks for College?

T he *New York Times* ran an article by Kevin Carey on March 8, 2015, predicting such big changes ahead for colleges, bringing an end of college as we know it. A flurry of reader responses followed on March 15, making different predictions. Since almost none of them mentioned the changes I would predict, I now offer my opinion.

Kevin Carey

Colleges have responded to their current popularity, mostly by building student housing and entertainment upgrades, presumably to attract even more students. What I am seeing seems to be a way of taking advantage of current low interest rates with the type of construction which can hope for conventional mortgages or even sales protection, in the event of a future economic slump. In addition, they are admitting many more students from foreign countries, probably hoping not to lower their standards for domestic admissions. They probably hope to establish a following in the upper class of these countries, eventually enabling them to maintain expanded enrollments by lowering standards for a world-wide audience of students, rather merely a domestic one. With luck, that might lead to

Ivy League

an image of superiority for American colleges, even after the foreign nations eventually build up their standards. The example would be that of Ivy League colleges sending future Texas millionaires back to Texas, which now maintains an aura of superiority for Ivy League colleges, well after the time when competing Texas colleges are themselves well-funded. The Ivy League may even be aware of the time when the Labor Party was in power in England, and for populist reasons deliberately underfunded Oxford and Cambridge. American students kept arriving anyway, seeking prestige rather than scholarship.

Wm. F. Buckley, Jr.

Television courses seem to be a different phenomenon. A good course is a hard course, so a superior television course will prove to be even harder. In fact, it might be said the main purpose of college is to teach students how to study; the graduates of first-rate private schools find college to be rather easy, providing them with extra time for extra-curricular activities which are not invariably trivial. I well remember William F. Buckley Jr, pouring out amazing amounts of written prose for the college newspaper and other outlets, in spite of carrying a rigorous academic workload. I feel sure he did not acquire that talent in college, but rather, came to Yale, already loaded for Bear. I am certain I do not know what future place tape-recorded classes will eventually assume, but I do feel such courses would be most useful for graduate students, who have already learned how to study in solitude.

To return to the excess of dormitories under construction, the approaching surplus of them might also lead to a better use, which is for faculty housing and usage. An eviction of students from dormitories would lead to urban universities beginning to resemble London's Inns of Court in physical appearance, with commuting day-students, mostly attending from nearby. The day is past, although the students do not believe it, that there is very much difference between living in Boston and living in California, and the much-touted virtue of seeing a new environment will eventually lose its charm. It may all depend on how severely a decline in economics resists the traditional pressure to escape parental control, but at least it is possible to foresee at least one improvement which could result from fiscal stringency.

http://www.philadelphia-reflections.com/blog/2930.htm

Net Neutrality

Bob Fernandez, a reporter for the Philadelphia *Inquirer* since 1993, recently addressed the Right Angle Club about Net Neutrality. He certainly knows his stuff about technology, but he got blind-sided, this time about politics. The term "net neutrality" is bewildering to most of us, and somehow it always had a ring of phoniness to it, as though it had been professionally synthesized by a corporate PR officer. And curiously, it seems to have much less interest to women, while it brightens up the eyes of almost any male audience. Men all have an opinion about it, even though the opinions differ from each other. Our speaker clarified this matter somewhat, by explaining that Netflix and Comcast have been dueling over this for several years. For one thing, Netflix consumes 40% of the bandwidth capacity of cable television.

In the commercial world, such a market dominance usually leads to the attitude by the customer (Netflix, in this case) that if they provide such a large amount of business, they are entitled to a volume discount. The seller, on the other hand, tends to feel that such a customer always wants special treatment so they can demand an extra-high price. The rest of the technical discussion is usually just special pleading, having to do with bandwidth, etc. The technical part was quite interesting, since the field is constantly changing, but it wasn't what they were really arguing about.

The next day's *Wall Street Journal* ran a commentary from the Republican member of the Federal Communications Commission, declaring technology had nothing to do with it. President Obama had instructed the Democratic majority of the commission to make cable television into a regulated utility, and Chairman Wheeler had complied. In an instant, the issue was no longer technical, but a Constitutional issue of whether the President has a right to over-rule an "independent" commission in its judgment of a technical issue. Since the Constitution never mentions Independent Commissions, it could become quite a tangled issue.

The *Wall Street Journal* also had a side commentary of its own. Quite a normal political squeeze job. Congress and Presidents love to impose irritating regulations, for the sole purpose of shaking the money tree. That is, inducing both sides of a controversy to donate campaign funds, dragging it out for a few years, and then letting the corporations run their business as they please. My, my. Such a cynical public we are developing. Maybe what we need is an Evita Peron, to do this dirty work in a smoother way, so characteristic of the female sex.

http://www.philadelphia-reflections.com/blog/2940.htm

Appealing the Constitution to a Higher Authority

According to Justice Robert H. Jackson, "We" (The Supreme Court) "are not not final because we are infallible, we are infallible because we are final." Scoop Jackson was the last Justice who never went to college or graduated from Law School, so his viewpoint concentrated on the

Justice Robert H. Jackson

practical outcome of a situation. In fact, the father of our constitution, James Madison, was learned in the history of many constitutions, and was well aware of allusions to divinity in the construction of our governing document, particularly when the sources of strong beliefs couldn't be grounded in evidence. The Constitution is an attempt to reconcile our culture to the needs of governance and the revelations of controversy. Composed by Enlightenment rationalists within a highly religious environment, the Founding Fathers were careful to use the metaphors of Religion, even though many were personally skeptics about the substance. Indeed, the Penman of the Constitution who ultimately wrote most of the words was Gouverneur Morris, a flagrant libertine. It had been the tradition of Constitutions to describe their culture by allusion to epic poems, drawing inferences about Right and Wrong from what had subsequently happened to ancient heroes after similar situations unfolded. Some would put the plays of Shakspere in that role in 1787, but the evidence is stronger for Roman writers, like Cato and Cicero. In my own view, this leap of faith was only divine in the sense it was a one-way street. A citizen might try to emulate the ancients, but appealing back to them was not likely to work.

Constitution

Although the Constitution can be viewed as bridging a gap between Culture and Common Law, or perhaps as placing a guardhouse between them, this relationship is not spelled out and therefore in theory might be changed. Other cultures, perhaps the native Indian, or the Catholic Church of Central Europe, might be substituted, or other legal structures resembling the Napoleonic Code might serve on the opposite side of the bridge. These substitutions were a legal possibility, but there is little doubt the American leadership intended for an Anglo-Saxon culture, linked with Francis Bacon's legal system, to prevail under a distinctively American flag. Because of our debt to France for then-recent assistance, there was once the possibility of French coloration to our culture, but the excesses of the French Revolution soon ruled that out. Some modern observers have capsulized the scene: First, we got the British to help throw out the French in 1754; and then in 1776 we got the French to help us throw the British out. Both our allies thought we played their game, but we were playing our own. The new Constitution specified no laws, but with little doubt the Framers intended the states to adopt British Common Law without the infelicity of saying so.

And then there is the Bill of Rights. Madison had great faith in the ability of structure (separation of powers, term limits, etc.) to command predictable outcomes, and initially resisted any need for a Bill of Rights. But the Ratification Conventions in the states showed him the need to yield. The First Congress soon enough confronted over a hundred proposed rights in petitions from the states, especially the four big ones. If anyone else had been in Madison's position, our Bill of Rights would resemble the European

Bill of Rights

one today, fifty pages long and growing. That outcome would have greatly weakened the Legislative branch, since after protests about Mother Nature subside, the legal fact emerges that Rights are merely laws which no majority can overturn. They might even be characterized as a contrivance for transient majorities to promote the permanence of their viewpoint.

Founding Fathers

But they are not the only contrivance in politics. Enshrinement of the Founding Fathers elevated their political positions into near divinity, whereas debunking the Founders personally undermines their symbolism as statues and myths. There was too much of this during the romance period of the Nineteenth century, but also in von Ranke's later marginalization of History into mere scholarship and footnotes, which was a reaction to it. The Founding Fathers themselves now supplant Achilles and Cincinnatus in our lexicon, and we have little choice but to accord more weight to their original intent in the Constitution, than to contemporary reasonings. Indeed, we are forced to acknowledge more similarity between George Washington's fictitious cherry tree than to his relations with Peggy Fairfax, when we interpret his thundering "Honesty is the best policy" in the second inaugural address. It is admittedly a difficult choice, but Justices now need to consider what his audience widely believed was his original intent, more than what later archeological discoveries uncover. Justice Scalia is correct in placing more weight on the original intent of the Founding Fathers than contemporary reactions to the same words. But in occasional conflicts between myth and reality, it seems safer to consider what the audience then widely believed, than what modern audiences would guess at.

http://www.philadelphia-reflections.com/blog/3075.htm

Millennials: The New Romantics?

Romantic Era

It was taught to me as a compliant teen-ager that the Enlightenment period (Ben Franklin, Voltaire, etc.) was followed by the Romantic period of, say, Shelley and Byron. Somehow, the idea was also conveyed that Romantic was better. Curiously, it took a luxury cruise on the Mediterranean to make me question the whole thing.

It has become the custom for college alumni groups to organize vacation tours of various sorts, with a professor from Old Siwash as the entertainment. In time, two or three colleges got together to share expenses and fill up vacancies, and the joint entertainment was enhanced with the concept of "Our professor is a better lecturer than your professor", which is a light-hearted variation of gladiator duels, analogous to putting two lions in a den of Daniels. In the case I am describing, the Harvard professor was talking about the Romantic era as we sailed past the trysting grounds of Chopin and George Sand. Accompanied by unlimited free cocktails, the scene seemed very pleasant, indeed.

Daniel Defoe

In the seventy years since I last attended a lecture on such a serious subject, it appears the driving force behind Romanticism is no longer Rousseau, but Daniel Defoe. Robinson Crusoe on the desert island is the role model. Unfortunately for the argument, a quick look at Google assures me Defoe lived from 1660 to 1730, was a spy among other things, and wrote the book which was to help define the modern novel, for religious reasons. His personal history is not terribly attractive, involving debt and questionable business practices, and his prolific writings were sometimes on both sides of an issue. He is said to have died while hiding from creditors. Although his real-life model Alexander Selkirk only spent four years on the island, Defoe has Crusoe totally alone on the island for more than twenty years before the fateful day when he discovers Friday's footprint in the sand.

But the main point of history was that Defoe was born well before William Penn and died before George Washington was born. The romanticism he did much to promote was created at least as early as the beginning of the Enlightenment, and certainly could not have been a retrospective reaction to it. Making allowance for the slow communication of that time, it seems *Robinson Crusoe* much more plausible to say the Enlightenment and the Romantic Periods were simultaneous reactions to the same scientific upheavals of the time. Some people like Franklin embraced the discoveries of science, and other people were baffled to find their belief systems challenged by science. While some romantics like Campbell's Gertrude of Pennsylvania, who is depicted as lying on the ocean beaches of Pennsylvania watching the flamingos fly overhead, were merely ignorant, the majority seemed to react to the scientific revolution as too baffling to argue with. Their reasoning behind clinging to challenged premises was of the nature of claiming unsullied purity. Avoidance of the incomprehensible reasonings of science leads to the "noble savage" idea, where the untutored innocent, young and unlearned, is justified to contest the credentialed scientist as an equal.

Does that sound like a millennial to anyone else?

http://www.philadelphia-reflections.com/blog/3186.htm

Passive Investing

Roger Ibbotson

Roger Ibbotson compiled the results of investing in the past hundred years, and divided it into different aggregate classes of investments – large capitalization common stock, small capitalization stock, bonds and whatnot. It happens that Burton Malkiel showed that such aggregates outperformed most mutual funds with the same goals, and John Bogle of Vanguard showed that index funds of such asset classes also outperformed stock-picker managed mutual funds, mostly because of lower costs.

Burton Malkiel

The eliminated costs included the cost of stock-pickers, who are often highly compensated, sales costs, and transaction taxes from frequent turn-over. He invented the term "passive investing" for the purchase of index funds rather than individual stocks, and it's easily understood why index funds would have lower costs than managed portfolios. Mr. Bogle's index funds in the Vanguard Group have an annual transaction cost of less than a tenth of a percent, while it is not uncommon for managed funds of common stocks to charge $250 or more, per trade. In a few years, index funds have grown to be half of the market, giving direct stock investing a very hard time of it. Buy them, hold them through thick and thin, and scarcely ever sell them. The consequence is that passive investing of this sort returns two or more percent more to the investor.

Vanguard Group

Multiplied by the compound income principles mentioned earlier, passive investing is pretty well sweeping the Health Savings Account field. In fact, most managers of HSA are having a difficult time deciding how to charge for other necessary services, like debit card management, sales, transactions, and advice. The most conservative of all small-investor vehicles, like money-market funds, bank certificates of deposit, and other savings vehicles, are currently suffering from such low interest rates that even they are being abandoned. In the peculiar financial environment of the present time, investors who shunned stock purchases as "gambling", find they have almost no other choice for their Health Savings Accounts. Investment management firms who depended on non-stock investments, are simply driven out of business if they don't switch to passive investments.

John Bogle

That's really all there is to say about passive investments for Health Savings Accounts, except to say it should be a good thing. Common stocks have out-performed just about everything else for a century. The small investor tends to be afraid of them because of the "black swan" crashes of 2008 and

1929, which students of the subject tell us occur about once every thirty years. We therefore should take a moment to address this problem, because various reactions to it, can have a very large effect on something the investor should be watching carefully, the percentage return on his investments. Multiplied by the compound interest effect of longevity, this is really the key to whether the HSA will be effective in lowering healthcare costs.

http://www.philadelphia-reflections.com/blog/3214.htm

Pickett's Charge

If you want to baffle a Philadelphian, just stop him and ask who defeated Pickett's Charge at the battle of Gettysburg. Like the Charge of the Light Brigade, everybody knows who the losers were, but nobody seems to know who won the battle. After all, history is usually written by the victor.

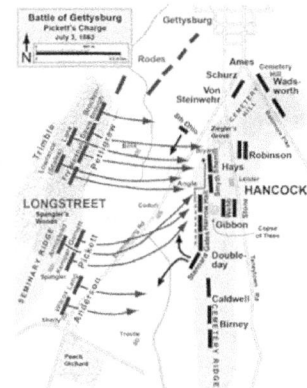

Well, in fact, the battle was won by 13,000 Union troops stationed at the Bloody Angle, only two soldiers deep behind a stone wall, to defend against 60,000 Confederate troops who had been

Pickett's Charge Map

concentrated by Pickett to converge on that point of defense. The whole Union army of about 60,000 men had been strung out along a farmland ridge, uncertain at what point Pickett would concentrate. At a little copse of trees at the angle of two stone walls, were three Philadelphia brigades, composed of Philadelphia blueblood officers and soldier volunteers drawn from Irish volunteer firemen, recruited by members of the Union League of Philadelphia. These Philadelphians, both officers and men, were to suffer 50% mortality in an hour of fighting. At one point they started to break and run when 150 confederate cannon were concentrated on their position, then rallied and held

their ground when it was the Confederate turn to break and run for home.

Although General John Gibbon was the highest ranking Philadelphian in charge, and Brigadier General Alexander S. Webb was a New Yorker who had been in command of the three brigades for only one day, winning the Congressional Medal of Honor, the real hero was Lieutenant Frank Haskell. Seeing the Union defenders starting to break, Haskell rode his white horse outside the wall ahead of his troops, and suddenly ordered them to turn and fire at the

Gen. John Oliver Gibbon hesitating Union troops. The shock of this maneuver stopped the retreat, turned the troops to face Pickett's onrushing men, and routed the Southern advance after Confederate General Armistead vaulted the wall and started to attack the defenders in hand to hand combat. A member named Haskell was in the audience when Author Bruce Mowday told this story to the Right Angle Club, but Robert Haskell never uttered a word.

Since this incident, I have repeated the story to dozens of Philadelphians, and not one was even faintly aware of it. It reminded me of Digby Baltzell's book *Boston Puritans and Philadelphia Quakers*, which expresses Baltzell's opinion that Quaker reticence is the source of Philadelphia's academic and political decline. My own opinion takes a different view of the distinctiveness of Philadelphia modesty, which was contrasted with New England by John Adams' remark that "In Boston, every goose is a swan."

Bruce Mowday

When you run your eye down the list of Philadelphia Union officers who fought in this crucial battle, there is only one recognizably Quaker name from a city which even at the time of the Civil War was still Quaker-dominated. Quakers had been urged by the London Yearly Meeting to withdraw from the war tax issues of the French and Indian, and Revolutionary Wars, but a great many Quakers had fought against the British, anyway. By the time of the Civil War, however, the antiwar Quaker position had considerably strengthened. I can still remember Henry Cadbury reciting the position of his mother, a satire of the Battle Hymn of the Republic: "He died to make men holy, we will <u>kill</u> to make men free." The Civil War had greatly strengthened antiwar sympathies in the North, especially in Quaker Philadelphia.

Revolutionary War

Consequently, when the spoils of war were handed out, public opinion demanded that the heroes of Gettysburg be rewarded, without drawing any openly negative opinions about those who declined to serve. After all, the Quakers had initiated and led the battle to free the slaves, and shared a certain amount of wide-spread sympathy with the idea that the Southern states were entitled to secede if they wanted to. And Quakers at the time retained considerable wealth and the power to defend themselves, if attacked, not to mention wide-spread ambivalence about the War. So, there was no great effort to persecute Quakers, but the idea of sharing the spoils of war with them, was just a little too much. Six hundred thousand soldiers had been killed in that war, and although Gettysburg contributed 51,000 of them, it was far from being the only bloody battle. It is my suspicion the constant decline of Quaker influence

Gen. JEB Stuart

in Philadelphia since the Civil War, can largely be traced to unpleasant echoes of this more or less inevitable response to a postwar commonplace.

It is unfair to bring up the subject of the battle at Gettysburg, without mentioning three other factors which historians cite as causes of the defeat of Generals Lee and Pickett. In the first place, the rather inferior Confederate artillery consistently overshot the target of the front line of Union troops, and fell harmlessly in their rear. Lots of noise, not much damage. It is also true Confederate General JEB Stuart was planned to attack the Union lines from the rear, but was delayed by attacks of troops under the command of, might you know it, General Custer. And finally, as Pickett himself remarked, "The Union Army probably had something to do with it."

REFERENCES

Pickett's Charge: The Untold Story. Author: Bruce E. Mowday ISBN:978-1-56980-4	Amazon

http://www.philadelphia-reflections.com/blog/3225.htm

Septa's Brain Center

The Right Angle Club was recently introduced to two important examples of the Philadelphia Scene. The old spirit we used to have so much of, capsulized by the expression, "Pick up the ball – and run with it!" It was very heartening to behold.

First of all, the speaker was the director of the Radnor Associates 21, a volunteer company making documentary films. Its headquarters is in Wayne,

SEPTA Nerve Center

across the street from the movie theater, in rather cramped quarters and a budget of $250,000 a year. Mostly run by volunteers and veterans of the old radio era of Philadelphia, they took it in their head it would be fun to make a video of the SEPTA nerve center, at 12th and Market. It's really pretty neat, with cuts and splices, telling the story of something most Philadelphians never dreamed existed. After all, the automobile revolution pretty well destroyed the old Philadelphia of trolleys and buses, subways and elevateds. Most people just drive to work oblivious to public transportation, vaguely aware blue collar Philadelphia has a network. One of the newer elements of the network is the high-speed line to New Jersey, which itself is thirty or forty years old. It takes twelve minutes to get from Haddonfield to Center City, so I take it; and thus had become vaguely conscious that SEPTA had greatly improved in the last couple of years. Everybody's polite and jolly, the trains and buses are new. And everything seems to run frequently, and on time.

In the legal community, there is a piece of interesting history about SEPTA. It was one of three parts of the old Penn Central, composed of freight, long distance rail, and commuter rail. In turn, this was a conglomeration of trolley companies, bus lines, freight and long distance rail companies. However mighty the old Pennsy might have been, it collapsed and consolidated, and then split into three parts. Only the freight lines really made much money and wanted to be set free of the national politics of intercity rail, the local politics of commuter rail, the union domination, and the whole image of "corrupt and contented". Well, the Conrail freight division is making a fortune hauling shale oil around, Amtrak is struggling to get subsidies from Congress. Where in the world is SEPTA, the commuter complex which always lost a lot of money?

Well, it has headquarters somewhere, and union dealings, and politics. But the engineering center is at 12th and Market, pretty much dominating the 13th Street exit of the Market Street subway, and the underground extensions of the tunnel connecting the Pennsylvania and Reading commuter lines. Nobody much goes there, except for the fact it is crowded with people, going somewhere.

Well, the director of Radnor got the idea of making a video of it, and if you get the chance to see it, it's quite remarkable as a film. More important than that, it shows someone got the idea of unifying the highly diversified hundreds of buses, trolleys, and trains in a nerve center. Every single driver of one of those vehicles is in video communication with headquarters, every one of those vehicles is tracked on GPM, every single switch in the system is controlled by a central operator. They watch to see how the weather is, where the crowds are, what the speed of the vehicle is, whether it's on time or not. And whether something needs to be re-routed somewhere to meet the rush, or the accident, or the weather. Not only whether a train is on time, but what its on-time record has been. Whether the vehicles and stations are clean, whether there's a hold-up somewhere. No doubt, they can tell whether someone is sick, needs an ambulance, and so on.

Now, this is SEPTA. I expected to see grumpy old union functionaries, growling at people. Instead, I saw the happiest group of blue-collar workers you can imagine, shouting out they have the best job in the whole world. Exciting and worth-while. There are lots of problems, so, great. More challenge, more variety. These are people working at all hours, and working hard. Happy. And the trains are clean and run on time. They are safer. Who cares what they do in St. Louis, or Tokyo, or Paris – we aren't competing with them, and we wish them well. This is Philadelphia, and these people are running with the ball. Including the director of the

Radnor studios, who decided, on his own, to give them a pat on the back. That's part of the spirit, too.

http://www.philadelphia-reflections.com/blog/3323.htm

Philadelphia Schools Success Story

As many know, we have a weekly lottery at the Right Angle Club, and the proceeds go to our favorite charity. I'm pleased to say our little project hit it big this year, and the executive director came back to us to report on the $120 million they raised this year. To remind you, this little charity was the imaginative idea of an anonymous donor, who wanted to know why our schools were so terrible – when not so very long ago, they were the pride of the nation. Was it the schools, or was it the students?

Random Scholarships Lottery

The experiment was to give scholarships to poverty areas, selected by random lottery, to go to private schools. After a few years, it became possible to see whether these students responded to the new schools, or not. Well, they did, by all sorts of measures. Remember, these kids were picked by lottery, and had all sorts of membership. Quite a few with Down's syndrome, for example. So, it was established that improving the schools was worth the trouble, and the money flowed in. If you have a really good idea, people will support it. In this case, it proved one thing conclusively: it's the schools that matter.

Now, I would have liked to see the money used to see whether it was most important to improve the principal, or the teachers, or what grade was best, or the street gangs, or racial mixing, or anything else anyone could suggest, whether you think they are bigoted or not. Now that we have a great experimental tool, let's experiment.

Well, the people who run the project decided to use the money to expand the schools, increase the number of scholarships, and strengthen the conclusions. They're probably right, because the money and the experience gathered together in this little charity did not originate with social scientists, or even politicians with a cause, but rather with some good-hearted folks who got enlisted into a project. So, while the scientists might want to let the bad schools continue to be bad so they could be studied in more depth, the people running the project, and probably the donors of the money, just wanted to make the schools better. So, they are concentrating on what they know, and they are closing down the proven bad schools. That's okay, too, of course.

If somebody else wants to prove something or test something-- let him raise his own money, to do so.

http://www.philadelphia-reflections.com/blog/3324.htm

Charter School Warfare

The Right Angle promptly invited Jason Mayland, school consultant, a second time, after he had mentioned the first time that Charter schools were "a whole different topic by themselves," during the first time he was here. The room was packed, and the intensity of the audience was something to behold. This is a very explosive subject, and most people doubt the full truth of what they have been told. All right, let's have it.

After all, most of us are old enough to remember when the Philadelphia public schools claimed to be the best in the nation, and Catholic parochial schools were also said to be the best. Right now, there is an uneasy feeling the deplorable state of the schools is responsible for much of the city's decline. There is a general opinion the schools are unsafe, expensive, and failing. It certainly is true the claim is being

Jason Mayland

made that they only need more money, at the same time they are said to cost $100, 000 per year for each teacher to produce deplorably bad results. It all goes to reinforce a general feeling in the public that this subject is important, expensive, obscure – and we are being lied to.

Our speaker did clarify one important aspect pretty quickly. We have about 40% fewer students than we used to have, which creates vacant school buildings and excessive pension costs from the past, a subject he referred to as "sunk costs." He wasn't sure why we had fewer students, but it's provable that we do, and by itself this issue would account for a large part of the dispute about how we can overspend and underpay the teachers at the same time. It's probably not the whole story, and it doesn't explain where the students went, or why. But it's a fact of the matter, and doesn't sound like a sort of thing which is easily fixed. It might even be something which more money could help, and with the passage of time, might get better just by attrition. With the city finances in bad shape, it probably isn't going to get city money, but the local discovery of oil shale might hold out some hope. Unfortunately, the people who live on top of that shale want to keep the tax revenues for themselves, and it is certainly true they are entitled to something after a century of poverty. A situation in which the rest of the state was supported by a Philadelphia surplus, whereas it has been true for decades that the rest of the state is supporting Philadelphia.

String Theory Charter School

About half the schools are now charter schools, but the difference in teaching quality is more controversial. Essentially, the parents say there is a big difference, and politicians are keeping their children from getting it. The teachers say the difference is very small, and the extra cost is very large. The proof of quality of teaching is difficult to obtain, and worse still is in the hands of the teachers themselves, who want very much to slant the results in their own favor. Even if they don't slant the results, they maintain the good students have been skimmed off, leaving them with inferior students. The rest of the arguments have the same quality: disputed results, and testy disputes. The rest of the Right Angle Club tended to agree with an earlier speaker that random scholarships show that private schools make a big difference, until we learned that Charter schools are not private, but part of the school system. So, let's repeat what we think we know: private schools would make a big difference for the kids, but maybe charter schools won't. If we could change the charter schools to be more like private schools in some way, perhaps we should do that. Since we don't know what the essential ingredient in private schools would be, perhaps the conversation should be between private schools and charter schools. Heaven forbid we change the public schools. If we could find out what the difference is, and put it in a bottle, we are ready to make the charter schools drink it. That's what the public schools are demanding, but after all these years of malfunction, their credibility is very low.

There's even another thing we could do. Every seventy years, perhaps we should change the political machine in charge of the city. Come to think of it, that would be about now.

http://www.philadelphia-reflections.com/blog/3376.htm

Pipelines to Philadelphia?

Since former Governor Tom Ridge stopped being in charge of Homeland Security, he has been running a lobbying organization in Washington. So when we asked him to discuss gas pipelines to Philadelphia, he sent us Ned Rauch-Manino. Ned promptly appeared, and made a very good case we ought to have a pipeline or two. One pipeline would run from the Marcellus shale area to Philadelphia, carrying raw material from the gas fields to the old refineries at Marcus Hook. And the other would run from the Atlantic Ocean mouth of the Mullica or Greater Egg Harbor Rivers to Philadelphia, carrying liquefied natural gas in ships built in Germany, coming from, well, he didn't mention where it was coming from. But it would be a second source of oil or gas, running up along the banks of the creek to Marcus

Hook, saving a couple hundred miles of travel. And incidentally putting those LNG ships next to the pine barrens of New Jersey, rather than right next to the city.

According to Ned, the liquefied gas isn't much of a hazard, because it would burn faster than its ice could melt, so perhaps the shortened voyage or the navigation up the Delaware River are more important issues. While such LNG might be coming from Africa or the Middle East, a more likely source would be South America. The kind of crude oil produced in Latin America will not suit very many of the American refineries, so new ones would likely have to be built. In the case of oil from the Arabian Gulf, the raw material is already suitable, but much of the present commotion is due to the Arabs using some of their own money to build refineries of their own. And much of the Arab civil war is an Arabian civil war. The only other major source of oil from that direction comes from the former Soviet Union. However, France is known to be sitting on top of a lot of oil and gas, which they leave unexploited for environmental reasons. In fact, the whole world seems to have a lot of unexploited energy sources, so the main issues are investment and know-how, not discoveries. Meanwhile, the Russians are doing their best to explore the Arctic basin. These oil guys are all big-time gamblers by their nature, so it wouldn't be surprising to find a lot of capacity is being built, just in case something turns up.

To return to the potential pipeline across Central Pennsylvania, the environmental issues look much different. Refineries were first built around Marcus Hook, in order to provide a return cargo for the railroads to the West, during the Nineteenth century. The New York and Baltimore competitors had to return empty, so the return cargo provided a major advantage. Sun Oil, which was the major pioneer of this effort, has since sold the refineries to other operators, who have not greatly prospered, however. Until, that is, shale fracking was discovered, and Warren Buffett bought the railroad complex. If you go down the Schuylkill on either the East or West banks, or the Art Museum, you find there has long been a network of rail lines hiding behind the bushes. Nowadays, those rails are filled with lines of brand-new tank cars. Freight runs at night, so most of us haven't noticed the oil trains. But they are there and they stretch for miles. No doubt, the rail lines will suffer if pipelines are built, but right now those railroads are running enormous profits. And they are right there, just a few feet from thousands of people. We haven't had a major fire or derailment yet, but other cities have, and the threat is a real one. This subject is definitely one to be continued.

http://www.philadelphia-reflections.com/blog/3377.htm

The New Jersey Constitution of 1947

The wording of the **1844** State of New Jersey Constitution concerning its Senate, is short and simple:

Article IV. Legislative.

Section I.

1. The legislative power shall be vested in a Senate and General Assembly.

Section II.

1. The Senate shall be composed of **one Senator from each County in the State**, elected by the legal voters of the Counties, respectively, for three years.

A century later, the state held another Constitutional Convention, in which the relevant sections in the 1947 Constitution concerning the Senate were revised:

Section II

1. The Senate shall be composed of forty senators **apportioned among Senate districts as nearly as may be according to the number of their inhabitants** as reported in the last preceding decennial census of the United States and according to the method of equal proportions. Each Senate district shall be composed, wherever practicable, of one single county, and, if not so practicable, of two or more contiguous whole counties.

By amendment effective December 8, 1966, an electoral commission was appointed to respond to changes in the census; search engines are currently not explicit about the senatorial redistricting between 1947 and 1966:

Section III

1. After the next and every subsequent decennial census of the United States, the Senate districts and Assembly districts shall be established, and the **senators and members of the General Assembly shall be apportioned among them, by an Apportionment Commission consisting of ten members, five to be appointed by the chairman of the State committee of each of the two political parties whose candidates for Governor receive the largest number of votes at the most recent gubernatorial election.** Each State chairman, in making such appointments, shall give due consideration to the representation of the various geographical areas of the State. Appointments to the Commission shall be made on or before November 15 of the year in which such census is

taken and shall be certified by the Secretary of State on or before December 1 of that year. The Commission, by a majority of the whole number of its members, shall certify the establishment of Senate and Assembly districts and the apportionment of senators and members of the General Assembly to the Secretary of State within one month of the receipt by the Governor of the official decennial census of the United States for New Jersey, or on or before February 1 of the year following the year in which the census is taken, whichever date is later.

2. If the Apportionment Commission fails so to certify such establishment and apportionment to the Secretary of State on or before the date fixed or if prior thereto it determines that it will be unable so to do, it shall so certify to the Chief Justice of the Supreme Court of New Jersey and he shall appoint an eleventh member of the Commission. The Commission so constituted, by a majority of the whole number of its members, shall, within one month after the appointment of such eleventh member, certify to the Secretary of State the establishment of Senate and Assembly districts and the apportionment of senators and members of the General Assembly.

3. Such establishment and apportionment shall be used thereafter for the election of members of the Legislature and shall remain unaltered until the following decennial census of the United States for New Jersey shall have been received by the Governor.

Article IV, Section III, paragraphs 1, 2, 3 amended effective December 8, 1966. (Emphasis added)

http://www.philadelphia-reflections.com/blog/3085.htm

Real Estate Mogul Urges Higher Real Estate Taxes

On Labor Day, 2015, the *Philadelphia Inquirer* featured a story on the masthead of its Business Section, to the effect a real estate tycoon had addressed a press conference that commercial real estate taxes ought to be raised. That's arresting news, of course, since real estate agents would be expected to oppose higher real estate taxes, no matter what. The argument he advanced was that adding 70,000 new jobs would be possible by upping the tax on real estate, but

Cheshire Cat Smile

the logic is not immediately obvious. It was related 14% of Philadelphia taxes come from real estate, whereas in New York it is 24%, in Baltimore it is 50%, and in Boston it is 68%. It's quite striking this is true, and perhaps it should be adjusted. But how does this help the real estate industry, and why would a real estate agent be agitating to hurt his own business? Why doesn't he act like every other agent for an industry does, by smiling like a Cheshire cat and pretending the point hadn't been made? As they say in Wall Street, every broker "talks his own book."

Gerard Sweeney

The newspaper goes on to report Mr. Gerard Sweeney, the CEO of Brandywine Trust is part of a campaign to change the state constitution to permit different rates for commercial real estate and residential real estate, something apparently not permitted at present. It's not clear why Mr. Sweeney believes the commercial tax would be raised instead of lowered, politicians being what they are, in what politicians often refer to as a "betrayal". But even if the "fix is in", it isn't clear why raising commercial taxes would increase city employment by such a remarkable amount. The argument is offered that raising taxes offends people, and employment can more easily move away than buildings and land can. Conversely, lowering real estate taxes ought to attract businesses to locate here, thereby raising employment. That argument has some force, when you are changing the historical relationships between neighboring cities, providing the historical difference has been large, and the new change is permanent. In fact, when a person whose short-term business effect would cost him money comes out in favor of a change, perhaps he really is making a credible point.

As a matter of fact, he is making a much stronger point than he seems to be. The issue he raises is valid enough, but its real application is to health insurance. It traces back to Henry J. Kaiser in 1945, discovering profitable businesses could make money by giving away health insurance to their employees. The explanation of this paradox is rooted in two anomalies: (1) most employee business taxes are based on the size of their income. The City wage tax is roughly 4% of salary, for example. The New Jersey Income tax is 14% of income. And (2) the effective corporate income tax is double the size of the individual income tax.

Henry J. Kaiser

Now, look at what happens when an employer gives health insurance to an employee. The tax is the same, whether it is on wages or on health insurance. But after a few years, fringe benefit is accepted as normal wage cost, so the wages in the pay packet fail to rise as fast as inflation. The consequence: pay packet plus insurance becomes the same total wage cost as pay packet alone would be. But the employer does not pay the other taxes he would have paid on the total, if it had not been reduced by the fringe benefits. Since health insurance premiums approach $10,000 annually, they are ordinarily the largest component of this tax avoidance. The employee might be $2000 better off, but because of the higher corporate tax rate, the employer is $4000 better off. For employers like Google who have 55,000 employees, the savings are great enough to consider moving the company, if another state offers a lower rate. And if someone protests most employers do not pay the top rate, this tax gimmick has a lot to do with it.

The tax structure needs to be adjusted, all right, but the City wage tax is the least of it. Corporate income taxes are too high, the corporations don't pay them, because of all the deductions they take. What's too high is the deductions.

http://www.philadelphia-reflections.com/blog/3378.htm

Abuses of Goodwill

The news section of the *New York Times* relates that Karthik Romanna, an Associate Professor at Harvard, has introduced an entirely novel idea about stock market economics. (The reason to emphasize the news section, is the *Times* rule that the Sunday Book review only prints reviews during the first week after publication release dates, a major reason for the pedestrian quality of that particular section. Reviews appearing in other sections, at still later times, may suggest experts in an obscure field have slowly waked up to something of significance.)

Even CPAs regard the work of the Financial Accounting Standards Board (F.A.S.B.) as boring beyond belief. But this 75-person non-profit organization in Norwalk CT makes the rules for what accountants do, and Romanna decided to take the time to figure out why corporations so regularly overpay to merge with other corporations. This looked like the place to poke around in the incentive system which FASB creates. After all, the price the acquiring stockholder pay is very large, and the fees investment banks pay to advise the participants are well-known to be generous. Both of these incentives push the price higher, but then the price the acquired company is paid pushes the price downward. A system of kickbacks paid to the acquired directors for cooperation would certainly be a factor, but perhaps not the dominant one. Romanna feels the standards for what corporations state is their earnings after the merger, may be more important. And perhaps there is also some momentum from the days of evaluating factories and heavy equipment, which once was fair, but now require a different standard of fairness for service companies with human services more to be reckoned in a sale price. Nevertheless, it creates uneasiness to hear that half of typical sale prices is now viewed as goodwill, allegedly based on projected future income. That sort of thing can quickly walk out the door in a recession, and seems likely to affect the opinions (and bids) of activist investors.

To settle the question of a fair price is above the pay grade of this reviewer. But it does seem entirely appropriate to challenge the present system and its rule-makers to make their reasoning clearer. And for shareholders of merger victims to demand to know why they should not be paid better. It is not satisfying for a pricing system which ought to be in constant tension, to remain too boring to discuss.

http://www.philadelphia-reflections.com/blog/3472.htm

Why is Capitalism Usually a Top-Down System?

"Trickle Down"

During the Great Depression of the 1930s, someone coined the phrase "Trickle Down" as a disparaging reference to how capitalism treats poor people. The implication lay in the choice of the word "trickle" instead of "pour", invisibly suggesting that rich people take care of themselves first, and poor people only get a trickle. By implication, a socialized system would start with designing programs for the poor, and if there is anything left, give a little of it to the undeserving rich folks.

Class warfare language is always intentionally divisive, but it works best during times of hardship, when even the richest people get a little worried about their future. Even so, it is a hard to reconcile with the spread of televisions and used cars among the poor, and is most useful when managers are confronting labor representatives for a larger share of profits, as contrasted with a larger share for owners. It's also hard to reconcile with free public schools for everyone, which frequently remain substandard because the teachers can't control the pupils, who sometimes prefer recreational drugs and a lifelong vacation from work. The problems of schools do pose a threat of creating a permanent underclass.

Samuel Gompers

Since a fair division of profit has never been precisely defined, Samuel Gompers defined the true position of labor as simply demanding "more". It's a little hard to deny that rich people are usually owners, not employees, with basketball stars and symphony musicians perhaps excepted. And it's also hard to deny that someone has to do the humdrum work, if risk-taking is going to remain attractive to those who have assets to risk. At times when interest rates approach zero, it becomes starkly apparent the penalty for unwisely investing assets, is losing your assets. That is, avoiding being poor is a major reason for trying to be rich. As lengthening longevity offers a fair opportunity for everyone to end his life with a thirty-year vacation, it clarifies everyone's thinking to imagine savings running out, while there still remains ample time to "enjoy" a vacation from work.

An esoteric way of looking at things is to realize that wealth creates credit. Credit is not debt, it is the unexploited ability to borrow, as first discovered by Robert Morris and Alexander Hamilton. It is often stated that banks create money by doubling it; it's probably more accurate that rich people double the value of their wealth by creating, but not using all of, their credit. It's spendthrifts and phonies who use it all. When someone climbs out of his Rolls Royce, you can't tell if he has used up his credit or not. But bankers know; you stop paying your bills on time if you have no credit left. Just about the only way an ordinary person can efficiently use his credit, is to buy real estate.

Robert Morris

So almost all stock market crashes grow out of an overextended housing boom. Mortgages are the main way to transform wealth into debt, and the rest just follows, even though you gradually pay down your debt and rebuild your credit. The crash isn't over until the debt is mostly re-converted into credit, which often takes a decade.

Alexander Hamilton

So while the punishment grows clearer with each additional year of idle longevity, the cause is not clarified that way. For whatever reason, some members of society are motivated to start businesses, even though those businesses are sometimes directed toward improving lifestyles which need little enhancement. A few entrepreneurs are able to fast-talk a loan from a banker, but generally speaking you must own some assets in order to risk those assets. Except for the extremely wealthy, such people choose between investing those assets to enhance them, and spending them without expanding their credit. Some do, and some don't; the difference may be hereditary.

A wise parent sees this coming, and steers his brighter children into the professions, his duller ones into the military, where recklessness is sometimes rewarded. A life in the sciences or arts is harmless, and may even have some utility. Some families prefer their children to go into the ministry or direct charities, and do not greatly object to sports, excessive drinking, or repeated marriages. But these families are depriving their children of better examples; the average family prefers hard work and diligence, savings and frugality. Not everyone can play polo well, or even marry a glamorous heiress, but almost everyone can work hard and perform a simple task for the less enterprising. Everyone can be frugal, if bad companions are avoided. It's not merely having opportunities, it's probably choosing which examples to follow that matters.

http://www.philadelphia-reflections.com/blog/3476.htm

New Views for the Economist?

The London *Economist* has a new editor, and a new owner. Mickelthwait, the old editor, is now working for Blumberg, and ownership has passed from one corporation to another. The two synchronous events may or may not have anything to do with each other, but the name of Rothschild has more or less vanished. No doubt the new management will change the cover page and format a little, but we must wait a little to see whether their editorial viewpoint has changed very much. A few token viewpoints will probably continue to be sacred, like support for American foreign policy, and admiration for the British socialized health system. But there is a sign, one change may be significant.

John Mickelthwait

Twice in the last few weeks, there has been a serious discussion in the magazine for serious economists, of the same newly-discovered fact. Whenever the private sector generates strong profits, the *Economist* sees strong evidence the majority of profits soon appear as increased credit in the real estate sector. Industrial profits transform into real estate investments, in other words. No explanation for this strange observation is offered, and perhaps it is just an observation, without a current explanation agreed by everyone. But after skipping that gap, the observation certainly has potential to explain much of the cyclicity of markets, offering an explanation why market upturns are so often followed by real estate crashes. And, if we are lucky, followed by some reasonable proposal for preventing such crashes?

If no one else is going to step forward with an explanation, let me offer one. For the small investor, real estate has long been the only available way to get into speculation on interest rates. A thirty-year mortgage starts with a small equity and a large debt, and gradually the borrower becomes a lender. Business schools teach that real estate is "where the rubber meets the road". But seeing a real estate boom, the rest of the market heads for the exits.

If that's the one-liner we are looking for, it probably neglects the last step. When wealth gets created, by a stock market boom or any other method, most small investors have discovered only one safe and comfortable way to participate. So, having temporarily exhausted that approach, they hesitate. During that period of hesitation, they build up an invisible form of wealth, called credit, which enables them to borrow where before that, they had no credit. The American discoverer of this puzzling concept was Robert Morris, the banker of the American Revolutionary War. And come to think of it, didn't Morris himself encounter bankruptcy and debtor's prison – from real estate speculation on credit?

So what's new? What's new is that longevity has increased to the point where it is sensible to liquidate the real estate and spend the proceeds on retirement. Having achieved lender status, they then aim to spend their last dime, on the last day of their lives. That seems just perfect, but where has all the credit gone?

http://www.philadelphia-reflections.com/blog/3473.htm

"Sir,"

In 1938 when I was 14 years old, I entered a new virtual country with its own virtual language. That is, I went to an eminent all-male boarding school during the deepest part of the worst depression the country ever had.

While it should be noted I had a scholarship, there is little doubt I was anxious to learn and emulate the customs of the world I had entered. My life-long characteristic of rebellion was born here, but at first it evoked a futile attempt to imitate. Not to challenge, but to adopt what I could afford to adopt. The afford part was a real one, because the advance instructions for new boys announced a jacket and tie were required at all meals and classes, and a dark blue suit with a white shirt for Sunday chapel. That's exactly what I arrived with, and let me tell you the green suit and brown tie were pretty well worn by the first Christmas, when I came home on the train for ten days vacation, and the opportunity to demand more clothes. As I remember, my disconcerted parents agreed to a new camel's hair jacket, for $10, which was also pretty worn-out by the following Easter vacation, permitting another campaign for proper clothes. Furthermore, the stigmatized "new boy" status was symbolized by requiring a black cap outdoors, and never, ever, walking on the grass. The penalty for not obeying the "rhinie" rules was to carry a brick around, and if discovered without a brick, to carry two bricks. But that's not what I am centered on, right now. The thing which really bothered me was unwritten, equally peer-pressured by my fellow students, the custom of addressing all my teachers as Sir. The other rules only applied until the first Christmas vacation, but the unwritten Sir rule proved to be life-long.

And it was complicated. It was Sir, as an introduction to a question, not SIR!, as a sign of disagreement. You were to use this as an introduction to a request for teaching, not as any sort of rebuke or resistance. Present-day students will be interested to know that every one of my teachers was a man; my recollection is, except for the Headmaster's secretary, the Nurse was the only female employee. The average class size was seven. Seven boys and a master. Each session of classes was preceded by an hour of homework, the assignment for which was posted outside a classroom containing a large oval oak table. Needless to say, the masters all wore a jacket and tie, mostly of the finest style and workmanship. They always knew your name, and always called on every student for answers, every day. Masters relaxed a little bit during the two daily hours of required exercise, when they took off their ties and became the coaches, but were just as formal the following day in class. I had been at the head of the class of what *Time Magazine* called the finest public high school in America, but I nearly flunked out of the first semester in this boarding school. It was much tougher at this private school than I felt any school had a right to be, but they really meant it. Over and over, the Headmaster in the pulpit intoned, "Of those to whom much is given, much is expected."

I had some new-boy fumbles. Arriving a day early, I found myself with only a giant and a dwarf for company at the dining table. I assumed the giant was a teacher, but he was a star on the varsity football team. And I assumed the dwarf was a student, but he was assistant house master. One was to become a buddy, the other a disciplinarian, but I had them reversed, calling the student "Sir", but the master by his first name. Bad mistake, which I have been reminded of, at numerous reunions since then.

When I later got to Yale, I began to see the rules behind the "Sir," rule. In the first place, all of the boarding school graduates used it, and none of the public school graduates, although many of the public school alumni began, falteringly, to imitate it. Without realizing it, a three-year habit had turned out to be a way of announcing a boarding school education. The effect on the professors was interesting; they rather liked it, so it was reinforced. The only time I can remember it's being scorned was eight years later, by a Viennese medical professor with a thick accent, and he was obviously puzzled by the significance. Hereditary aristocracy, perhaps. Indeed, I remember clearly the first time I was addressed as Sir. I was an unpaid hospital intern, but the medical students of one of the hospital's two medical schools, flattered me with the term. In retrospect, I can see it was a way of announcing their medical school knew what it meant, while that other medical school was just red-brick. Although they too had mostly graduated from red-brick colleges, their medical school aspired to be Ivy League.

If you travelled in Ivy League circles, the Sir convention was pretty universal until 1965, when going to school tieless reached almost all college faculties, thus extending permission to students to imitate them. Perhaps this had to do with co-education, since the sir tradition was never very strong in women's colleges, and denounced by the girls when the men's colleges went co-ed. Perhaps it had to do with the SAT test replacing school background as the major selection factor for admission. Perhaps it was the influx of central European students, children of European graduates for whom an anti-aristocratic posture was traditional, and until they came to America, largely futile. Perhaps it was economic. The American balance of trade had been positive for many decades before 1965; afterwards, the balance of trade has been steadily negative.

In Shakespeare's day, "Sirrah" was a slur about persons of inferior status. In Boswell's eighteenth Century day, his *Life of Johnson* immortalized his characteristic put-down with a one-liner. It survives today as a virtually text-book description of how to dominate an argument at a board-room dispute. "Why, Sir," was and remains a signal that you, you ninny, are about to be defeated with a quip. It's a curious revival of a new way of immortalizing small-group domination, and a very effective one at that, which even the soft-spoken Quakers use effectively. Whatever, whatever.

The tradition of addressing your professor as "Sir," is gone, probably for good, except among those for whom it is a deeply ingrained habit. Along with the tradition of female high school teachers, followed by male college professors.

http://www.philadelphia-reflections.com/blog/3471.htm

Health Savings Accounts: Brief Extracts for My Friends

New blog 2015-12-16 18:33:50 contents

http://www.philadelphia-reflections.com/blog/3478.htm

Supreme Court Rescues Obamacare, June 26, 2015

The case of *King v. Burwell* was argued before the United States Supreme Court March 4, 2015, and the decision was reported June 26, 2015. In a clear victory for President Obama, the Court held that it was not the intent of Congress that a phrase in the statute, even though repeated six times, should be the final meaning of the law. Someday a participant in the writing of the law will come forward and tell the story of how the words got into the statute in the first place, but at the moment all we know is the words are there, and the law is unworkable if they remain. Just about everyone would agree these two statements are true. Furthermore, it is clear only Congress could change them, and Congress has changed parties since they were originally written; so they probably cannot be changed at all before new elections are held, unless the President agrees with Congress to do it. There is a third possibility: Congress and the President could make private agreements about what they would compromise on and present a friendly adjustment. Whether that was tried and failed, or whether it was not tried at all, is unclear. So, the Supreme Court did what it never wants to do, it changed the law.

Since millions of citizens had watched (on C-Span) the legislation, dropped on the desks of astounded Congressmen, with no opportunity permitted to debate or amend it. Indeed, even to read most of it before it was voted on, the public is inclined to take the Court's word for it, that...

"The Affordable Care Act contains more than a few examples of inartful drafting".

Whether the clause in question was accidental or not, is a matter of opinion. The clause in dispute reads, and is repeated six times, as

> **Tax credits "shall be allowed" for any "applicable taxpayer", but only if the taxpayer has been enrolled in an insurance plan through "an Exchange established by the State under [42 U/S.C., pp18031]" pp36B(b)-(c)**

Some idea of the Court's historic position is given in a few quotes:

> "In a democracy, the power to make the law rests with those chosen by the people. Our role is more confined – to say what the law is." – Marbury v. Madison, 1 Cranch 137, 177 (1803)

> "Oftentimes the meaning – or ambiguity – of certain words or phrases may only become evident when placed in context." – *Brown and Williamson*, 529 U.S. at 132.

> "Reliance on context and structure in statutory interpretation is a 'subtle business, calling for great wariness lest what professes to be mere rendering becomes creation and attempted interpretation of legislation becomes legislation itself.' – *Palmer v. Massachusetts* U.S. 79, 83 (1939)

In the end, three conservative Justices, Scalia, Thomas and Alito found there was no reason to change the language of the statute as ambiguous, and four liberal Justices, Ginsburg, Breyer, Sotomayer, and Kagan found there was. The two swing Justices, Kennedy and Roberts, joined the liberals in finding the statute ambiguous, for a final vote of 6-3.

Judging from the global circumstances, it is probably fair to conclude that ambiguity was probably not the only issue involved, and it was probably inartful for the Court to establish a precedent that such a restructured role for the Court was either necessary or desirable. The history of Canada's use of this device to coerce provinces into joining the national health system was well known in Canada at the time. And the McCarran Ferguson Act has restricted insurance administration to a State level for seventy years. Both of these examples would seem to have provided a sounder basis for the Court to interfere in what really seems like pretty clear language in the law.

http://www.philadelphia-reflections.com/blog/3250.htm

The Pity of It, Iago; Employer-basing is Mostly a Tax Gimmick

Times change. The Japanese have been defeated in "the" war. The spirit of sacrificing anything else to survive an external threat has subsided. California has become a blue state, and is fast becoming a minority-dominated one. A new generation has appeared, and unmindful of historic beginnings, has come to accept old expedients as simply the rules of the game. In particular, fringe benefits are no longer a bonus, but just a part of earnings which for some reason are tax-sheltered.

To sum it all up, Chief Financial Officers no longer feel they are cheating when they maximize tax "benefits". It's legal, isn't it? Obviously, an employee receiving a big gift finds it more welcome than paying for it himself, especially since it is tax-free and other people don't get the same treatment. Economists who have examined the matter are fairly unanimous that fringe benefits are all soon merged in the minds of employers and employees alike as "employee cost." Within a few years in a competitive environment, both sides of the gift soon treat fringe benefits as only a tax benefit, with comparable reductions in the pay packet to adjust for them. The cost of the gift soon equilibrates, only the tax deduction is a true transfer.

Nevertheless, there are economic limits, if not legal ones. Issues like Portability, Job-Lock, pre-existing conditions, and individual choice would disappear if health insurance were freed of linkage to employers, since these issues are all traceable to the mandatory link between health insurance and losing your job. We really do have an employer-based system, but it has a price. Lifetime healthcare insurance policies would place considerable strain on portability and choice, so employer-basing stands in the road of multi-year insurance. Maybe, just maybe, we should reconsider the advantages and disadvantages of having it remain a gift from employers. The growing suspicion it has been the main impetus for cost escalation is worth testing.

In fact, the shareholders usually get a bigger gift than employees do. State and local corporation taxes vary, but a profitable corporation pays 38% federal corporate tax, and the total corporate tax burden approaches 50% if you include mandated sharing of other fringe benefit costs, the highest in the developed world. By defining fringe benefits as a tax-deductible cost of doing business, some major corporations effectively increase their net income by half.

To understand how that is possible, just look at any payroll tax stub next payday. All these features were intended to redistribute wealth, but the CFOs, turned them into shareholder advantages. Tax deductions from the pay packet total about 15% of net pay. But the employer must match most of that deduction with his own contribution, which brings him to 30%. And furthermore he pays twice as high a tax rate: about 40% tops compared with a blended individual rate of 15%, so it all adds up to 60%. Let's use the imaginary example of a $10,000 health insurance premium, where the employee gets a $1500 tax reduction, but the employer gets $3000. It's after-tax money, so the employee effectively gets $1726 and the employer $4200. For a big employer, multiply that by 10,000 employees and you get a noticeable amount of money. It's so much money you can imagine what the stock market would do, if a proposal to abolish it looked as though it might be enacted. But would you believe it – that's not the worst of the situation.

The worst is – the employer has been given a very large financial incentive to raise the cost of healthcare. The higher the better, and shareholders ought to love it. Physicians have the same incentive, because we would love to raise our fees, as Adam Smith so tersely put it in *The Wealth of Nations*. But at least we doctors took the Hippocratic Oath, and most of us are a little ashamed of this conflict of interest. Whereas, a stockholder controlled company has hired a manager with the mandate, to make as much profit as he legally can. Let's summarize: we have engineered a system where it is well known among CFOs that you can often make extra profits by giving a gift of health insurance to the employees. And if that isn't a tax gimmick, I don't know what would be. We have finally reached the point where the health system costs 18% of Gross Domestic Product in spite of closing 500,000 mental health beds, all of the tuberculosis sanatoria, all of the polio beds, and lengthened human longevity by thirty years. Maybe you can blame that paradox on doctors, but I doubt it.

We have simply got to stop telling fairy tales about Henry Kaiser and Liberty ships eighty years ago. This is a tax gimmick and it has to stop. I would be happy to meet with the Business Roundtable to discuss how we could stop it without crashing the stock market, but it has got to stop. My two-part proposal is pretty short, however:

> **Proposal:** Employers should discontinue providing free health benefits to their employees, at the same time corporate income taxes should be capped at the same rates as individual income tax. The speed by which this is to take place might be determined by the Federal Reserve in response to economic conditions, but in no case longer than three years to complete the process.

The competitors deserve a word, here. About half of business is made up of big business, and half is small business. Wall Street and Main Street, if you will. The opportunities which Henry Kaiser stumbled upon in 1943 mostly apply to big business, and probably much of that anomaly can be traced to the fact that bigger businesses are more likely to be profitable, and more likely to be engaged in international trade, where competitors don't get a vote. Some of the tax benefits for small business like Subchapter S, probably represent an effort by Congress to help domestic competitors without helping foreign ones.

But self-employed people, and unemployed ones, are excluded. Very likely, much of the politics of healthcare is intended to help these people, without helping small business or big business, and without helping foreign competitors. Pretty soon, you have a tangle of interests affected by removing the obvious tax inequity which Henry Kaiser is given credit for discovering. Just about everybody has something to gain, something to lose. So it begins to be impossible to say, on net balance, how much the country would be improved by abolishing it. That's particularly true, with the Affordable Care Act on trial.

Just how bad things are, is hard to say. But plenty bad enough. We know about job lock and the other features directly attached to employer-based insurance, and we decided to live with them. But the escalation of healthcare costs, and the soaring international debts used to pay for them, are becoming too much to handle. We can tolerate a lot of things, but it's not clear we can tolerate 18% of GDP devoted to healthcare, particularly if the price keeps rising. It's hard to imagine anything people would prefer to spend their money on, than on longevity. But when serious people, or at least people who take themselves seriously, start talking about euthanasia as a solution to our health cost problem, you know the costs are starting to hurt. So get this: you can only do it once, so euthanasia isn't as useful a solution as tax reform.

What a Tangled Web We Weave. For the most part, only economists are familiar with the rather well-established fact that wages in the pay packet soon decline to recognize the value of other items in the total wage cost. In this case, it is the 15-20% tax reduction as a result of the Henry Kaiser tax dodge. After eighty years, news of this theory has seeped into the minds of labor unions, and is slowly becoming common parlance among union membership. So inevitably, bickering about tax subsidies for poor people gradually reached the same point of recognition. Negotiators who have won an economic victory on an esoteric point, often find it difficult to restrain their boasting of it afterwards.

In the case of subsidies for the poor to pay for national health insurance, the subsidy was based on whether the individual's income was a certain percent of the poverty level. When the individual's income falls in the border zone, it may make a big difference whether or not to include the tax deduction as wages. A decision on this point affected eligibility for subsidy of millions of low-wage employees of big business. And that in turn affected their personal decision whether to buy health insurance in the exchanges or to continue to get it through the employer – which way would be cheaper? With millions of dollars at stake, it is small wonder the negotiations apparently broke up and agreed on a two-year postponement of including employees in Obamacare. Since the political makeup of Congress had changed since the law was passed, the law itself could not be adjusted to smooth out this difficulty. The implication (pretense?) has been circulated that somewhere buried in legislation there exists some relief from this situation, but it will not be effective until 2018. It scarcely seems likely a useful compromise could be devised during that time window, or during a Republican administration afterwards, so stay tuned.

A related issue might also be involved in the mysterious revival of the minimum wage by union politicians. It seems possible the reasoning is that, since you can't lower the threshold for subsidies, perhaps you could raise wages to meet the threshold. Some pretty sophisticated people are apparently advising these politicians about a pretty obscure economic point. Ordinarily, the market wouldn't tolerate such manipulation, but having gone off the gold standard, perhaps it now seems possible to give it a try. All in all, the arguments for a minimum wage are so tenuous, it seems more likely that inflation is being toyed with, as a possible way to expunge indebtedness.

http://www.philadelphia-reflections.com/blog/3256.htm

What Obamacare Should Say But Doesn't

1a. **TAX EQUITY.** All tax exemptions stimulate overuse, because they amount to a discount. For example, federal tax exemptions now mainly extend to two consumer purchases: health insurance and home mortgages. We currently have national crises in both at the same time. The tax-subsidized home-mortgage housing bubble played a major role in the 2007 financial panic, while **tax-subsidized health care** threatens to lead health costs into a second **unsupportable bubble**. Higher education seems to be going the same way, and it becomes difficult to imagine what would result if two or three of these bubbles merge. The expression "Children playing with matches" comes to mind. Giving a tax advantage to one group but not to its competitors is essentially just a variant, containing the paradoxical advantage that the competitors will object to it if they can't extend it to themselves.

Giving a tax subsidy to employees but not to self-employed or unemployed persons nevertheless created a uniquely American system of **employer-based health insurance**, and lobbying now perpetuates this rather odd system. Noting the allegedly temporary origins of this tax quirk (as a wartime expedient), merely dramatizes its lack of justification for seventy years afterwards. It should not be necessary to describe collateral damage like job lock and internal hospital cost shifting. The issue of equal justice alone should be enough to justify the abolition of this unfairness. To mandate individual coverage but differentially exclude large subpopulations from tax exemption, is to invite a Supreme Court case. And since such a law has been passed, the sooner a damage case is granted *certiorari*, the better.

> *"If health insurance is mandated, its tax treatment must be uniform."*
>
> **HIDDEN COST**

To achieve equity, it does not matter whether tax exemption is given to everyone, denied to everyone, or limited to part of the cost (reducing the exemption for some, partly extending it to those who do not have it). Any choice between these three would make it equitable, although gradual elimination would be better, still.

Once the tax is equalized, this proposal clears away the main obstacle to

1b. **INDIVIDUAL OWNERSHIP OF HEALTH INSURANCE POLICIES**, already proposed in Congress; but seemingly without hope of adoption. Determined opposition from the current owners of "self-insured" groups, the employers, or the unions who have acquired this function from employers. Since most such arrangements are *de facto* "administrative services only", insurer protests of higher administrative costs for individual ownership are often just relics of ancient combat between Blue Cross and commercial insurers.

Regardless of the internal structuring of incentives, healthcare reform cannot be permanently settled without individual ownership. It must be understood, however, that eliminating the tax preference could be resisted at first by patients who acquire it, because of fear the eliminated tax would in some way be shifted to them. That need not be true, if consideration is given to the relative size of the losers and gainers. Since the membership of group policies greatly outnumber individual policy holders, the redistributed revenue cost of tax equity would be considerably smaller than 50/50. The CBO should provide a sliding scale estimate for negotiating purposes.

1c. **ENCOURAGE WIDE-SPREAD DIRECT MARKETING** OF HEALTH INSURANCE. Since Health Savings Accounts and Catastrophic High-Deductible Health Insurance are libertarian ideas without religious overtones, it is uncomfortable to advocate them as mandatory, even passing laws to that effect. However, libertarian doctrine does not seem to preclude creating incentives to universal adoption. This doctrinal attitude imposes slower adoption than mandating them, although a better product results from more trial and error as the idea spreads. Therefore, readers may be surprised to see me advocate electronic insurance exchanges <u>as a way to speed up trial and error spread of the idea's adoption</u>. It is a way of preserving flexibility of deductibles, benefits, alternative uses of surpluses, and vendor arrangements. It is also a way of narrowing the conflict with the Tenth Amendment, combining state regulation with inter-state marketing. If multiple alternative details prove necessary, direct computer marketing would be a quick way to discover what the permissible alternatives would be. Finally, the wide spread examples of other interstate marketing can be employed to search out how to *convert* marketing from intra-state to interstate, rather than assume certain commerce is inherently (and permanently) interstate or inherently within-state.

An accidental feature of Health Savings Accounts is that the account can be growing for a number of years before the re-insurance feature is frequently needed. Indeed, young people may need a certain form of reinsurance protection, and a different form as they grow older. The important feature is to have permanently stable savings vehicle in place while different forms of re-insurance are proving themselves. It seems heresy to say so, but we might even discover niches of the marketplace where first-dollar coverage or service benefits have some useful temporary role.

1d. PRE-EMPT STATE LAWS WHICH INHIBIT CATASTROPHIC COVERAGE. State mandated benefits now severely limit high-deductible insurance in many states, and are the main reason Health Savings Accounts have been slow to spread. The provisions of ERISA shield employer-based health insurance from the unfortunate health coverage mandates in question. ERISA could not have been successful without this pre-emption, so unions and management unite in absolute concern to isolate ERISA from congressional meddling, although for different reasons.

1e. REVISIT McCARRAN FERGUSON ACT. This act effectively makes the "business" of insurance the only major industry restricted to state rather than federal control. It should be amended to **permit the sale and portability of health insurance policies across state borders** and interchangeability of individual policies when people change state residence, thus greatly increasing competition and reducing prices. Once more, present law discriminates in favor of the employees of interstate corporations, who are also exempted by ERISA.

1f. MANDATE DISPLAY OF DIRECT COST MULTIPLES NEXT TO PRICES (FEDERAL PROGRAMS ONLY) (whenever prices are displayed, as in bills, price lists, etc.) FOR ITEMS COVERED BY HEALTH INSURANCE. Some high mark-ups are justified, but the public has a right to criticize them. This would not prohibit, but would considerably hamper, cost-shifting. It should be presented to provider groups as forestalling the prohibition of cost-shifting because of abuse. For this and other reasons, it would enhance provider competition.

1g. REIMBURSE HOSPITALS ONLY ON RECEIPT OF ASSURED POST-DISCHARGE HANDOVER OF MEDICAL RESPONSIBILITY (FEDERAL PROGRAMS ONLY). Unfortunately, hospitals do need increased incentive to improve post-discharge communication, which now increasingly occurs on a Saturday. Payment by diagnosis, otherwise a seemingly attractive idea, results mostly in sequestration of medical charts within the accounting department. That's undesirable at any time, but is most destructive at the vulnerable moment of hand-over.

1h. Similarly, REIMBURSE HOSPITALS FOR LAB WORK ON THE LAST DAY OF HOSPITALIZATION ONLY AFTER DEMONSTRATION IT HAS BEEN REPORTED TO A RESPONSIBLE PHYSICIAN. Such lab work, frequently obtained within hours of discharge, is sometimes overlooked and may even be unobtainable for the previously mentioned reasons, which in this case also apply to the hospital's own physicians.

1i. RESTORE ORIGINAL FORM OF PROFESSIONAL STANDARDS REVIEW ORGANIZATIONS (PSRO). These physician organizations effectively regulated many issues which are now the subject of complaint. They were lobbied into ineffectiveness in 1980, and together with "Maricopa", essentially turned medical oversight over to insurance companies who thus receive no physician advice except from their own employees.

1j. **ENCOURAGE THE ESTABLISHMENT OF REGIONAL BACKUPS FOR AMBULANCES DRAWN OUT OF AREA.** At present, ambulances are limited to going to the nearest hospital, rather than to the hospital of patient preference. The main justification for such behavior is the possibility that a second call might come while the ambulance was in a distant area. Fire departments have long solved this problem by shifting reserve vehicles into an overstrained area, to cover that area while the home vehicle is temporarily unavailable. In some areas, a reserve vehicle backup might require additional ambulances, but mostly it requires a mobile phone network. In areas of extreme distances between ambulances, the main need would be to relax regulations which exclude volunteer vehicles from serving that function. In densely settled urban

> *"Treat liabilities like debts. And transfers from the general fund as liabilities."*
>
> **ACCOUNTING, FOR CONGRESSMEN**

areas, we now have the preposterous situation of mothers in active labor being stranded at the wrong hospital, only a few blocks away from the obstetrician who has their records. When such situations are repeatedly encountered, the current IRS exemption from financial reporting should be rescinded from the ambulance sponsor.

1k. As a general principle, when a service, device or drug is used in both the inpatient area, and the outpatient one has its price exposed to regular market forces in the outpatient arena, the same price should be applied to it in the inpatient arena. It would be sensible to add a (separately negotiated) inpatient overhead adjuster reimbursement which generally applies to inpatients, and a second adjuster for the emergency room. There will be some services which are totally unique to inpatients or emergency rooms, which will have to be treated as outliers. In this way, a mutually reinforcing restraint is placed on such dual-use items – with the market holding down outpatient costs, and the DRG ultimately holding down inpatient/emergency costs including outliers. As a general rule, the overhead cost-multiple established for dual-use, should apply to the single use items of either in-patient or out-patient. The key to all of these balancing limits is to permit open competition between hospital emergency services and private competitors, and an absolute prohibition of linkages between providers and emergency vehicle operators. After a brief

> **"The Supreme Court Needs Help, Too"**

trial, all such price constraints should be exposed to re-negotiation with an eye toward establishing transparent regional norms.

2. **LEGISLATE OVER-RIDE OF 1982 MARICOPA CASE.** This unfortunate U.S. Supreme Court 4-3 decision, was never tried and upholds only a motion of summary judgment about a *per se* violation. It prohibits physician groups from agreeing on lower prices, and has been taken to mean physicians are excluded from exercising control of HMOs and Managed Care. It also perpetuates the notion of individual competitors in a profession which is rapidly acquiring larger groupings as units of competition. By some quirk, the full tape recording of the 1982 U.S. Supreme Court arguments can be heard on the Internet. It is "above this author's pay grade" to know whether it would be better to ask the Supreme Court to review its earlier decision, or to make legislative changes in the antitrust law which would somehow result in a better outcome.

http://www.philadelphia-reflections.com/blog/1730.htm

Steve Brill: Healthcare Without Insurance Companies

Stephen Brill has written a very professional description of the "Inside baseball" of the Affordable Care Act, from the decision to go ahead with it, through the turmoil of ramming it through Congress, to the badly mismanaged introduction of the insurance exchanges. At the conclusion of this largely critical description entitled *America's Bitter Pill*, Mr. Brill devotes fifty pages to his own proposal for a better system.

Stephen Brill

Essentially, the proposal is for large hospital chains or multi-hospital groups to merge with, or otherwise take over the function of, health

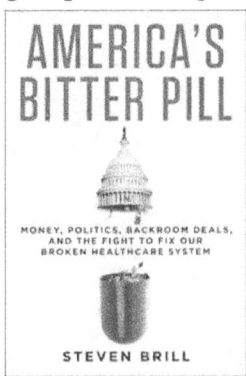

insurance companies. And, indeed, there is one little paragraph buried within the Source Notes which seems to be adequate justification for that idea. It's a quotation from a January 5, 2014 article in the *Journal of the American Medical Association* to the effect there were 831,000 American physicians in 2011, compared with 1,509,000 health insurance employees. The question it raises is plain enough. Why does it take twice as many employees to manage the insurance, as it takes physicians to deliver the care? Surely, a great deal of money could be saved by reducing the health insurance cost, and Mr. Brill's proposal is to let the hospital conglomerates take over the insurance industry.

An important truth is stated, but this particular conclusion is too drastic because it would strip the public of its normal expectation for impartial decisions between two counter-parties. At least, for rare and expensive disputes it would; many other problems need fixing only because employer-based insurance created them. It redefined many small risks as big ones, mostly in response to unwarranted lobbying to extend unwarranted tax dodges. But extending the expendable argument to include what insurance does well (spread the risk of low-volume, high-cost unpredictable expenses), requires proof that other institutions would do it better. I am reluctant to give up catastrophic health insurance, while admitting the rest of current health insurance is too costly and expendable.

Bill Gates & Warren Buffett

Others have said the same thing, and no doubt the health insurance industry will mount a defense. My own proposal could be twisted to mean something else, except my way of saying it is that individual patients should take over much of the non-insurance insurance function, by using Health Savings Accounts, and thereby reduce their net costs by passive investing in index funds. Since Obamacare was probably only a first step toward something else, replacing health insurance with governmental solvency assurance may have been in the President's mind. But any way you massage the message, there is an essential contribution by insurance which probably cannot be adequately replaced. Anybody at all could suddenly develop a huge medical expense, and be unable to pay for it. The chances of that happening are small, so the cost per person is also modest. Ignoring exceptional cases like Bill Gates and Warren Buffett, everyone needs a catastrophic insurance plan. No proposal for general use is probably workable without "stockholder risk in calculated balance with customer risk-taking". My own succinct criticism of Obamacare is that it has made Catastrophic health insurance illegal for everyone over the age of 30. If a feature like that is essential to ACA success, its own future is doomed, in my opinion.

Theodore Roosevelt

In a sense, the whole thing the matter with the existing system of employer-based insurance is that it boxed itself into a corner of first-dollar coverage, and only modestly retreated from it. That is, instead of initially insuring the worst health disasters with lowest premium cost, and progressively lowering the deductible as people could afford it, the Health Insurance industry did it in reverse. It started out with insuring the cheap stuff before it reached expensive stuff. No wonder one President after another, starting with Teddy Roosevelt, proposed some kind of reform. It's far too late to assign the blame for this misjudgment of the past century, but it is not too late to confess the error and re-design systems with the hope of fixing it. Yes, it is true it would have been cheaper to address the issue thirty or forty years ago, but meanwhile the thirty-year extension of longevity during the 20th Century has a good side, too. The essence of our problem is that, right now, it is whatever it is.

http://www.philadelphia-reflections.com/blog/3144.htm

Savings Accounts: Visions for New Prosperity

Yes, it's true, I have written and published a book, to be released November 1, 2015 as a review copy. It's called *Health Savings Accounts: Planning for Prosperity*, with general distribution to follow as soon as the printer arranges it. As the title suggests, it has new slants on a program I helped invent in 1981, plus revised visions for the future. It was not written as a political pamphlet, although six candidates for President have endorsed HSA as their healthcare platform, so it's inevitable it will receive partisan treatment.

SYNOPSIS. As John McClaughry of Vermont and I originally envisioned it, the Health Savings Account was to have two parts: A tax-exempt savings account, plus a high-deductible ("Catastrophic") health insurance policy. Its purpose was to extend income tax deduction to that half of insured subscribers who were not employees of companies which gifted the insurance to employees. Seventeen million people have subscribed up to January 1, 2015, and about a million more are added every year, so far depositing 24 billion dollars. But it's still not fully tax exempt.

In the early years, I suspect **tax-free investing** in high interest savings was the attraction for many. (HSA happens to be the only retirement fund, tax-deductible both when you make a deposit, and when you make a withdrawal.) When interest rates declined from the 18% level, I suspect attraction shifted to its convertibility at age 66, to an IRA (Individual Retirement Account), so you might then **overfund it** to an annual limit of $3350. You can then use the augmented surplus for retirement income, unless you get sick and die, first. HSA doesn't give subsidies to poor people, but then neither does the Affordable Care Act. The ACA merely takes tax money and distributes it to poor people. Health Savings Accounts could easily do the same, if the government would relax its monopoly of charity care. High-deductible health insurance is required but is not tax-exempted, as it would be, if HSAs were permitted to pay the premiums on behalf of the owner. That feature lacks only a one-line amendment to the HSA enabling act. Perhaps deductible-flexibility would be another good addition. A friend of mine has a $25,000 deductible policy for a $460 premium. That illustrates: **the higher its deductible, the lower its premium.**

That describes **Classical HSA**. In the book I propose several additions for new needs in a **New HSA**. Life expectancy was 47 years in 1900; today it's 84. Compound interest has longer to work; investment techniques are far cheaper. For a century, long term investments in the stock market have yielded 11%. Subtracting 3% inflation, net return for passive investment in total-market index funds is 8%. To be safe, we estimate 6.5% returns, which make it double every ten years, so you can do the math in your head. From age zero to 90, it doubles nine times, to **289 times its original size** (2, 4, 8, 16, 32, etc). While past experience won't guarantee future performance, this sounds as safe as you can get. If the stockmarket drops 50%, you're still far ahead. The investment potential of Health Savings Accounts produces new dimensions of safety and yield. Throw in health insurance, and you get yourself quite a deal.

Increased longevity offers other surprises. Grandparents become a reality instead of a legend in their families, sickness migrates from workers to retirees. That's not entirely good, because the sick can't earn, while those earning money increasingly don't get sick. That's a remnant of 1930 employer-basing. Health insurance has become a huge transfer system, top-heavy and politically vulnerable. When one third funds the other two-thirds of anything, look out for revolts. I propose Health Savings Accounts as a vehicle to transfer funds between ages without pooling them, either from grandparents to babies, or babies to grandpa. Savings accounts retain individual ownership while earning income. Compound interest curiously rises over time, assisting forward transfers. Transferring backward from older to younger, requires skipping forward in generations. It's too involved to explain in a brief synopsis, but that's the idea. Three hundred fifty dollars at birth could become $350,000 at age 90. If Obamacare would pay for itself, Savings Accounts could take care of everybody else for $175 at birth. If you don't privatize Medicare, it only costs $87.50. Linking pieces together, the individual can transfer money from one stage of life, into another where he spends it. It's his money, and only government can allow it or prevent it.

There are two flies in this ointment. Financial middle-men will resist being displaced. And employers will regret not being Santa Claus. Some adjustments must keep us from shooting ourselves in the foot. There's even a larger goal than this, possibly too much to take on just yet. We might start consolidating the pieces into **Lifetime Health Savings Accounts, based on the whole-life insurance model**. That industry finds the model greatly superior to term life insurance, and more profitable. Its design is similar to that of a consolidated health payment industry, but might take decades to perfect. But it's a goal, and not a political one unless we make it so. In a population of 350 million, the potential savings, and other effects, are pretty staggering.

http://www.philadelphia-reflections.com/blog/3437.htm

Early History of Health Savings Accounts

I soon persuaded the American Medical Association to endorse the plan, John Goodman of Texas wrote a popular book about HSA, which persuaded Bill Archer, the chairman of the House Ways and Means Subcommittee on Health to push a law through, enabling a pilot program. Today, the nonprofit Employee Benefit Association reports 11.8 million people have Health Savings Accounts, mostly in states without mandatory small-cost coverage laws to hamper the use and pricing of deductibles. Others report a third more. One clarifying example would be mandatory birth control pill coverage, which not only undercuts the purpose of a large deductible, but is politically inflammatory as well. Health Savings Accounts are popular in Indiana where Patrick J. Rooney was a heavy early supporter, but HSAs until lately were almost unknown in New York and California, which had extensive mandatory small-benefit laws, sometimes dozens of them. Today, to my amazement, California leads the fifty states in HSA enrollment, and JP Morgan Chase services 700,000 policies.

http://www.philadelphia-reflections.com/blog/3272.htm

Concept Behind New Health Savings Accounts

At present, the Classical variety of Health Savings Accounts is reported to have 15 million subscribers and 25 billion dollars deposited. It seems to be growing at the rate of a million new subscribers a year. Let me confide it is very satisfying to discover 15 million people are intrigued enough to commit money to an idea John McClaughry and I put together thirty years ago. It happened without any money of our own devoted to promoting it, and from which John and I have derived no personal gain. I have an eventual goal, which requires some legislative help to get going. It's called the Lifetime Health Savings Account. It builds on the original idea of the year-to-year Classical HSA, but follows the whole-life insurance plan, so familiar to purchasers of life insurance. It is, to lifetime health care, what term life insurance is to whole-life. A single lifetime marketing effort, internal professional investing of its float, early overfunding followed by later distribution of surpluses.

However, you can't buy lifetime health insurance right now, and won't be able to, until certain laws are modified. Furthermore, the various steps will take decades to come together into a unified lifetime demonstration. Therefore, two strategies were tried out. The first was to omit some steps, and work around The Affordable Care Act as if it didn't exist. That's easier on paper, called the New Health Savings Account (N-HSA), but takes just as many decades to prove itself, and is forced to surrender much of the financing cushion which gives it a safety factor. Therefore, it is only included in the book to display some of the hidden technical features which tend to make it workable. These details are then extracted like pearls from oysters, and strung into a necklace of ideas. The eventual outcome is the last chapter of the book, which is able to refer to these pearls as if the reader was familiar with them. Which he will be, if he reads the book sequentially, and which he can be, if he refers back to the sources in other chapters in other guises. The result is a description which is quite simple, but each feature of which has explanations which are not entirely self-evident.

If I started over and re-wrote the whole book, it would be much smoother. However, I made a conscious decision to sacrifice that feature, in order to get the book into the national debate in time to make an impact. Even now it seems a little late, while many fast-breaking events just have to be ignored because there is no time to include them.

Meanwhile, I decided two things: to go ahead with the book with its final goal largely sacrificed to immediate needs. And, to prepare an interim, or new, Health Savings Account proposal. The new proposal would go ahead with a few advances toward Lifetime Health Savings Accounts which might be acceptable enough to political combatants to pass Congress, but which could advance the concepts of Lifetime HSA through some experimental stages. Even that proved too ambitious, because It would require decades to prove the concepts that way. So it was stripped down some more, creating the last chapter of this book. Instead of taking a few ideas and struggling with them for a lifetime, I finally came to the view that a lifetime was a series of events, some of which worked out, and some didn't. Like a string of beads, I finally strung them together, recognizing that some would have to be replaced. s essentially a pilot study of proof-of-concepts, preparing the way for more grandiose plans after most demonstrated flaws had been cleaned up. I called it New Health Savings Accounts (N-HSA), and thought it would work to include all of healthcare except for age 21-66. Although that would cover 58% of health costs, it would not conflict with the Affordable Care Act, and might eventually seek greater compatibility as the ACA evolved. If the ACA got thrown out, it would be a concept prepared to take its place, without tumbling us into healthcare chaos. But until some upcoming elections clarified where the public stood, the two ideas could essentially stay out of each other's way.

A description of N-HSA follows in this section. Because the calculations of the Lifetime goal-model showed L-HSA could generate considerably more money than required, I was misled into thinking abbreviated N-HSA would generate ample funds. That turns out to be only narrowly true, and it has such a thin margin of safety that a major war or a major recession would probably sink it before it had enough public support as a pilot study. That didn't stop Lyndon Johnson from going ahead with a program which was only 50% funded, together with a Social Security program which has a similarly bleak balance sheet, and a Medicaid program which is a notorious failure to do a good job, or to come close to paying for itself. But those were different times. In 1965 the international balance of payments of the United States had been positive for 17 years in 1965, but has been steadily negative for fifty years subsequent to that time. It shows no sign of improving. The Vietnam semi-revolution destroyed Lyndon Johnson's political career in the Sixties. His entitlement programs lingered on as unsupportable public generosities for fifty more years, but they simply must change if we are to survive as a nation.

The Health Savings Account is based on a different set of fundamentals. We have saved enormous sums by stamping out thirty diseases, but at a different sort of cost which has increased as we extend our generosity to essentially everybody, even non-citizens. We have created a tidal wave of rising expectations which even the most optimistic surely cannot imagine can continue indefinitely, and a rising rebellion of envious foreigners with nuclear capability, and an unstable monetary system without any definable standard; which puts us at the mercy of ambitious foreign rulers. And yet, we continue to throw huge amounts of money at research, in a typically American mixture of hope and calculation. We have narrowed most medical costs to about five chronic diseases, cancer, Alzheimer's, diabetes, Parkinsonism and self-inflicted conditions, and we aren't going to stop until those five conditions are cured. Nobody told us to do such a thing, but everybody secretly hopes it will work. If we eliminate diseases, well, everybody can then afford not to pay for them. Unfortunately, it created a bigger, unanticipated, problem.

We bifurcated medical payments into three compartments: working people age 21-66 who earn almost all the new wealth, but mostly don't get very expensively sick. Secondly, the elderly from 66-100 who don't earn much money, but increasingly have all the expensive diseases. And third, the children from birth to age 21, who only consume 8% of the health care costs, but who have no opportunity, either to pre-fund their costs, or to earn enough to pay for them. This third group, as I found out, unexpectedly upset almost all plans for comprehensive care, cradle to grave. Rich and poor folks, about whom we have heard so much, are distributed within these three groups. What we have mindlessly created is the need for an enormous transfer of wealth from the people who earn it, to the rest of the nation, who have most of the disease and little of the earning power. This wealth transfer is just more than the generosity of the country can comfortably support, and it's been growing steadily from President Teddy Roosevelt to President Barack Obama.

My concept, right from 1980 onward, has been to find a way for individuals to store up their own wealth while they are working, so they can support their own costs when they grow older. Doing it by demographic classes is too much altruism to tolerate – just listen to what young people are saying about their lucky elders, and to what the baby boomers are saying about the millennials. The nick-names will change, but that's the way all interest groups talk about each other. I had assumed that medical science had already reduced the disease burden to the point where self-funding your own old age – in advance – would cover a majority of the population, but I now have to admit we are only part-way. Enough volunteers would probably support N-HSA to make the experiment a success in normal times, but it doesn't have enough cushion to be completely confident it could survive a war or a depression. Every time we make a scientific advance, the day of feasibility gets a little sooner. So, it boils down to whether you are willing to take the risk now, or not. I'd like to see a pilot study of volunteers iron out the kinks, first. But a great many impatient people are boiling to take the risk right now, and if we are lucky on the international and economic level, it might work. Every bull market "climbs a wall of worry." If we approach it more gradually, it is more certain to work. Judge for yourself.

http://www.philadelphia-reflections.com/blog/3316.htm

New HSA for children

That results in no small effort, however, because our focus programs require a transfer of at least 68% of healthcare costs from people who are not seriously sick, to the places where costs more naturally concentrate. That is the case for every broad-based plan ever proposed, but this is the first one to concentrate on nothing else, because we are blocked from diluting them with the costs of well people. Since we cannot force well people to agree to funds transfer, we merely relieve them of the need to pay the costs, and expect they will take advantage of the opportunity. Similarly, we cannot force sick people to make use of the program, so we must rely on their recognizing the advantages.

First Year and Last Year of Life Coverage. We start with the simplest case. Everybody gets born, everyone dies; there are no exceptions. Furthermore, these two years are the most expensive ones, and likely to remain so. Medical advances of the future may raise the costs of terminal care, but even that is uncertain, and the costs may go down. And it is likely to remain true that just about everybody who dies, dies at the expense of Medicare, so we start with firm data, readily available. To simplify boundary disputes, using the calendar dates of the first year and the last year eliminates that particular fuzziness. Furthermore, obstetrics and terminal care contain elements found in no other age groups, concentrating the scientific issues. When I first presented the idea to a medical audience, one wit rose to the microphone and recalled a town in Pennsylvania that passed a law stating: "Every fireplug in the town must be painted white, ten days before a fire." He was of course quizzing me how you knew when the last year of life began. The answer is, you wait until the person dies and count backward, and you get the cost data from Medicare. Since everyone knows how imprecise hospital costs may be, it is probably better to reimburse average terminal care costs for the year and the region. If the patient retains Medicare coverage, a simple funds transfer to Medicare simplifies both administration and coverage disputes.

The big problem is the long transition, unless Medicare and the Administration should agree to prime the pump. Therefore, the program must remain voluntary, and may even have waiting lists at times, depending on its popularity. Certain tricks known to financial managers may help to shorten the transition to self-sufficiency. For example, CSS reports that the first year of life absorbs 3% of healthcare costs, and the last year about 6%. That is, $10,000 should be more than ample for the first year and $20,000 for the last year of life. By externally supplementing the first, the surplus after ten years can be applied to accelerating the funding of the last year. But even doing that could take twenty-five years to complete the process. Funds could be borrowed with a bond issue, of course, but eventually that would raise costs and prolong the transition. "Sweet spots" can be found, but at the best, the transition is a long one, certainly spanning several turnovers of political power. Nevertheless, at the end of it, these pivotal medical coverages would acquire a major funding source, and other programs could experience a major reduction, up to 9%, in cost duplication.

In this, as in other parts of the book, we round off investment returns to 7% when we really expect only 6.5%. Using the old adage that money doubles in ten years at 7%, the reader can verify approximate accuracy by doing the sums in his head as he reads.

The Rest of Childhood, Seniority, and Permanent Unemployability. So that was the first **Proposal 21:**, to which the second one is a natural extension. All children are dependents of their parents, and the heavy costs of obstetrics (magnified by the unusual concentration of malpractice claims) make it impossible to devise pre-funding schemes. Young parents are often strapped for funds, so the lack of pre-funding is a growing problem in a Society uncertain of its family structures. Therefore, we have devised the grandparent roll-over. Tort reform would improve but not eliminate this work-around. Therefore children are lumped with senior citizen costs, and hence to a buy-out of Medicare.

The permanently unemployable are included by using surplus funds from the other two, mainly because there is no way to establish eligibility except by starting a program and seeing what it costs if you monitor it. Those may not seem like adequate reasons to lump them together, but it will be seen the details feel congenial, to do so. That is always a good sign in new proposals.

Multiple Programs in Multiple Years. The transition problem is always vexing in a new program, but reaches some sort of new limit when the ambition is to work toward uniformity and maximum patient control, across the entire nation; fragmentation always sounds easier. The temptation is always there to order and threaten to use force, but it must be resisted. Furthermore, enormous cost savings are readily available if programs are multi-year, and cost is a paramount issue, here. It's hard to beat compound interest, the longer the better.

We explain the reasoning of the grandpa transfer in the next section. It's simple (one grandchild's worth of costs per person), it uses surplus cash after a grandpa has no further use for it, and it comes at an optimum time on the compound interest curve. It greatly stretches the lifetime for compounding, but it is readily suited for a limitation on perpetuity. It even follows established family patterns, although families are under considerable stress, these days. True, it jumps over a new barrier for the first time, but it doubles the duration of compounding, skips over the issue of leaving a dark hole around Obamacare, skips over the issue of pre-funding obstetrics, simplifying a host of unnecessary red tape obstacles. And it reduces costs by half.

No Employer Involvement, No Obamacare Contributions. At first, it seems like a relief not to have to deal with the two thorniest issues of the past, but in fact it doesn't quite do that. If the patient has duplicate coverage, there must be cordial negotiations to see which coverage should be dropped. And while significant savings can be readily demonstrated, there will be some residual revenues which have to be transferred along with the patient or the new program will starve. The complicated systems we have evolved to facilitate cost-shifting will probably invalidate old statistics, and perhaps some old ideas. Transferring six percent of the gross domestic product is by definition a tedious, difficult task, even if you reduce it to four percent in the process. Everyone is hesitant to name the individuals who will lose their jobs, or their pensions, or their seniority, if the program shifts significantly. But if the savings aren't significant, what good are they?

http://www.philadelphia-reflections.com/blog/3374.htm

The First Year of Life, Leading to the Rest

Locked Savings

We have already discussed how relatively easy it would be to anticipate the average medical costs of everyone's last year of life, put the money into a securely locked piggy bank, and gather interest to help pay for that dreadful last year in the same way whole life insurance pays for funeral costs. One hard part is to keep Congress from dipping into the lockbox, or the Federal Reserve from robbing its real value by allowing inflation. However, if protecting the Lifetime Escrow can be presented as financing everyone's health into old age, the public might well rally to it. Any agitation necessary to defend the piggy bank might by itself be a boon to reminding the public what is at stake for them. By comparison, generating the funds might actually be the easy part.

But what about the first year of life, whose expenses have already been spent? (The term is loosely applied here to include pregnancy and post-partum, plus pediatrics). The concepts are introduced of pre-funding terminal care, paying off the debts of getting born, and current-funding the long healthy stretch through most of life. The proposal is to merge it all after transition steps taking decades, fully recognizing that some people will have to pay twice for having been born, and some will never pay for having to die. Indeed, in any insurance plan there is some unfairness in order to remove risk. First, get the terminal care fund established and funded, showing benefits in the first year or two as proof of the concept. Then, start collecting additional contributions to the terminal care fund for the moral debt each citizen has for his early childhood costs, and do it for perhaps ten years. Add this money to the terminal care fund, but make its finances as visible as if they were separate. Meanwhile, keep chipping away at the maternity and childhood costs of litigation. The first chip is to recognize that malpractice costs are disproportionately concentrated in this group, so the fund would greatly benefit from tort reform. Vaccine costs are also strongly influenced by liability costs.

One subordinate goal is to present the cost of childhood as partly a score-card on progress in tort reform, broadly defined, ultimately rallying the public to restrain itself in the jury box. The mechanism would be to dramatize the disproportionate concentration of these costs by local and national aggregation, letting the newsmedia speculate on the variation.

Finally, it should be said that the Health Savings Accounts are a vastly more flexible way of paying for health care than using the service benefits approach, at a time of great flux in the system. These accounts are described in greater detail in subsequent sections, but the main advantage at this point is to translate fund transfers to money without service benefit attachments, to make unification and substitution more plausible.

To some degree, service benefits are in conflict with indemnity benefits, in a manner resembling the conflict between debt and equity in the banking sphere. The best one can hope for is to shift the location of the interface between service benefits and indemnity, bringing the friction out into public view, and equalizing the power of contending sponsors. Therefore, the best place to present the issues is to regard DRG diagnosis groups as service benefit subsets, and outpatient costs as aggregated indemnity. But one of the main mistakes of the DRG system was to extend it to every hospitalized inpatient. This is particularly important in situations where the diagnosis has no relationship to a particular length of stay or average cost level. Inpatient psychiatry should be paid for as if it were an outpatient service, and chronic diseases such as Alzheimer's disease should be excluded from DRG as well. Emergency room visits should also be separated into two groups, depending on whether the patient is subsequently admitted to the hospital.

We started by saying these issues should be chipped away, during the period when more pressing issues are being addressed head-on. The first and last years of life are disproportionately expensive, so they need special attention to cost reductions. But the list of other small issues is a long one, providing ample opportunity for trade-offs within ambiguous opportunities. The main goal of these new proposals is to redirect cost-shifting perceptions from something to escape if possible, into a vision of advancing sensible provision for your own risks at a different age. The notion of generating investment income is not a small part of the notion of prudent behavior.

After this short treat, of a long-term vision, we now return to more practical short-term proposals. The heart of them is the Health Savings Account, but several preliminary features must be explained in advance.

http://www.philadelphia-reflections.com/blog/2474.htm

Buying Out Your Medicare?

The public is vaguely aware there is a problem with Medicare indebtedness, but for the most part this issue is swept aside, for fear agitation might injure the chances of funding healthcare for those of working age. The size of this debt is not well known, but can be guessed at by realizing Medicare costs are 50% borrowed. The current CMS data show a line for contributions from the general fund, equaling 50% of the total. Because cost accounting for government accounts has its special features, inter-agency transfers are referred to as assets. It's a debt, all right, and a large part of it is owed to the Chinese. For whatever reason, Treasury debt is entirely "general obligation", so it is not usually possible to tell from Treasury debt, how much is assigned to particular debts. They would have to be totaled from Medicare annual reports, which are not generally available for much of the past. So we don't – right now – know how much we owe foreigners for Medicare debts; but it is considerable, very likely going back to the days when deficits began to appear. That gives me a choice: I can keep quiet about the subject, or I can conjecture. I choose to conjecture.

Some, maybe all, of the transfer from general taxes in the latest year to Medicare, was borrowed. Medicare started in 1965, but during the early years the receipts from payroll deductions were larger than the expenses of the Medicare program. But when the program was fully underway, it ran a deficit. For how many years, and for what amounts, is only a guess. But I assume guessing the debt to be equal to a full year of Medicare expense, is large enough to make the point I wish to make, but may well be larger. For present purposes, let us assume the existing debt is equal to a full year's cost of Medicare, which we do know is 549.1 billion dollars. This guess is selected for illustration because it is large enough to cause alarm, but is probably on the small side. I hope it will provoke some official figure to be released, and sincerely hope my own proves to be too large..

Because, if it proves close to the guess, it presents a future problem for paying off the debt, which would actually be worse than the healthcare cost now under such heavy debate. The past indebtedness is currently not under debate, and is still getting worse. The public, including my colleagues in the medical profession, often point to Medicare with admiration. Since everybody likes a dollar for fifty cents, that's perfectly natural. And so it is also perfectly natural for elected officials to treat the matter of replacing Medicare as if it were the "third rail of politics." Just touch it and you'll be dead. That's also fair play, until it is proposed the whole medical system of the country be covered with a "Single Payer System", which is a fancy way of proposing everything should be funded like Medicare; and that's just too much.

So I propose, discomfiting friend and foe alike, that we buy our way out of this problem by allowing the public to buy its way out of Medicare. One by one, as they approach the 65th birthday, they should have the opportunity to relinquish Medicare, by depositing $80,000 in a

Health Savings Account. Assuming 10% compound income return (see Chapter Four), $40,000 should generate $433,000 by the age of 91, which I assume to be the average longevity in a few years. By taking a guess at the size of the debt, the remaining $40,000 would throw off an additional $433,000 for paying it off. With 25 million Medicare recipients paying that much, let's hope it is more than adequate right now, although it will clearly become inadequate if we delay. These numbers ought to seem like a bargain to the public, and they certainly would seem like a bargain to the government. If there is any other proposal for managing this debt, we have yet to hear it. That's probably because of "third rail" concern, but unfortunately it may also reflect there is no other solution to talk about.

Issues and Problems In the first place, $40,000 at 10% will only yield $202,000 by age 83, the present average longevity. It will slowly grow, as will the medical expenses from 83 to 91. The debt is already too conjectural to justify more precision, but a decade or so is not unusual for oriental negotiations. Sooner or later, we must expect this progressive longevity to flatten out, and make the problem harder to solve.

In the second place for a long time to come, people arriving at their 65th birthday will have a history of payroll deductions when they were young. This will eventually dwindle down, but it begins as a quarter of Medicare costs, and must be returned as part of the buy-out. Meanwhile, persons older than 65 will have fulfilled their payroll deduction, and are paying annual premiums, which also equal a quarter of Medicare costs. This seems to be approximately prorated, so only the payroll deduction is owed these people during the transition.

And to go on, there will surely be medical developments. Some of them may raise costs, some lower them, and all of them summarized by a hoped-for cure for cancer, which may raise costs or lower them, more likely raising them before eliminating them. Once the discovery is made and announced, its price will be known, and appropriate adjustments demanded. For this and a host of similar issues, only a scientific body with the power to adjust prices can be expected to make the appropriate response with mid-course corrections. Given the present affection of the public for subsidized Medicare, it appears likely, voluntary buy-outs will be a slow and protracted process. They should provide ample time for basing reasonable adjustments to what would be mainly favorable developments.

http://www.philadelphia-reflections.com/blog/2749.htm

HSA Lifetime Payments: Limits of Feasibility

The two traditional ways to pay for healthcare are paying directly with cash, or paying indirectly with insurance. Each has advantages, and we return to them later. This book proposes a third payment method which ought to be cheaper, while medical care itself ought to be unaffected. The payment idea grows out of a quirk of modern health care: Children up to age 20 consume only 8% of current medical costs; 92% of healthcare expenses arise decades later. Most families of young people could save up money during the long low-expense period, adding extra compound interest to use later. If this approach reduces overall costs, some of the saving could be used to subsidize the poor. No one doubts some extra interest could be gathered. The really critical question then sharpens: Is it enough to be worth the trouble?

The calculation is not an easy one. In the past century, the nature and cost of healthcare changed dramatically, and will change more in the future. Nevertheless, attempts are often made to estimate national health costs; lifetime costs are now widely accepted to range around $350,000 per person, in year 2000 dollars. Women cost about $50,000 more than men. That's partly a result of the statistical convention of attributing all costs of pregnancy to the mother, and it also reflects females living longer than males. These are daunting amounts of money, but at least we can estimate some upper limit to costs from them. At the other boundary, we know some interest could be earned on almost any balance. So the problem has a solution. The real feasibility issue is whether it produces enough savings to be worth the trouble.

The ability to save varies considerably between families, interest rates vary, longevity increases; no one can know precisely what health care will cost when newborns of today live to be a hundred. On the other hand, estimating national totals is often easier. Dividing national data by the size of the population generates individual averages, which are more natural to comprehend. Furthermore, sometimes we know the available revenue but not the costs. It seems a little cynical to say so, but since one limits the other, they are often (roughly) interchangeable. The rest is a little speculative, and sometimes you just have to make an educated guess.

What a hypothetical average person could afford to pay is one of those speculative matters, and what the average person would willingly pay is even harder to guess. But there are limits to reasonableness; some boundaries can be recognized. So, let's now test what the plausible limits might be, starting with a range of interest rates. As a further preliminary, present longevity is to age 83, and one plausible guess about where it might go next century is age 93. The limit to what almost everyone could afford for a newborn child is guessed to be $500; it seems to be a bargain the government would readily accept as a subsidy to the poor, in order to cover a $350,000 expense. Table # 1 displays the first stab at an estimate. It leads to a conclusion: the proposal of pre-funding health care seems feasible enough under certain circumstances, to justify further investigation.

Interest Return According to Roger Ibbotson, the acknowledged authority on investment statistics, inflation has closely approximated 3% per year for the past century. United States stock market assets have appreciated in a range from 10% (large cap stocks) to 12.7% (for small-caps) for a century. Growth stocks and value stocks have followed different cycles, but over a span of a century have generated almost identical returns. This table makes the hypothetical assumption that average parents already contribute as much as they can at the birth of their child, and all further additions to the child's fund are investment income. Can the cost of a lifetime of health care be supported by a $500 contribution at birth? Under certain imagined circumstances, the answer seems to be a tentative "Yes" – if the fund can be invested at 7 to 8%, or the average longevity is between 83 and 93 years. Although it may take a little explanation, these do not seem like unreasonable expectations. It might therefore be said that if there are no interruptions or withdrawals (a totally unreasonable expectation by the way), the presently expected cost of an average lifetime of healthcare could be accumulated from the investment of $500 at birth. With no further expenditures than the original $500, although it may be a little too early in the discussion for a skeptical reader to accept that. How about this for an alternative: Although the devil is most assuredly in the details, the goal of paying for a substantial amount of healthcare in this way, is at least conceivable.

Having said that, it should also be firmly stated that paying for *all* of healthcare costs this way, is neither necessary nor probably even desirable. In the first place, when you make things totally free, they lose their perceived value in the eyes of the recipient. He treats the gift as worthless, and is induced to spend money even more carelessly than he does with insurance. Secondly, by placing a cap on the upper bound, we adopt indemnity principles of shifting the risk to the person in control of them. It thus removes the temptation to favor inflation as a way of escaping from debts. Third, the explanation acquires specific numbers to replace vague promises. So, let's set the far more realistic goal of paying for half of it, and seeing if that seems even more feasible by using somewhat reduced limits.

The achievement of $175,000 cannot be made by simply cutting one of the ingredients in half, because that reduces his balance (and its resultant later income) by half, also. The result is the recipient soon gets into a downward spiral, just as the miraculously enhanced income sent his spiraling balance upward. We develop a family of curves (figures 2a to 2d) for different contribution levels in the next chapter, but must first digress to meet an unexpected development. There's a sweet spot, and we are already close to it. To test this point, we have some very rough estimates from the AHRQ (the Agency for Healthcare Research and Quality) of the distribution of average health costs by age. If we subtract these costs from the data already mentioned, we would choose 8% as the most likely income, and age 88 as the most likely average longevity. The results are seen in Graph #1, and summarized in Table #2. To assist in the verification, the AHRQ data show that 8% of costs are in the age group 0-20; 13% in age 21-39; 31% in age group 40-64; and 49% are over 65. The preliminary results are seen in Figure 1a.

Whoops! It is immediately obvious our preliminary description has forgotten something important. We will correct the graph in a minute, but first we must explain something about paying for healthcare. All of the revenue for healthcare must be generated during the working years of, roughly, 18 to 66years of age. Ignoring a few trust-fund exceptions, the costs of childbirth, neonatal costs, and childhood are currently borne by the parents of a child. To some extent, the fall-back costs of the grandparents are also covered by people in the working age group. To go even further, when government pays for dependent healthcare, this too is covered by taxes, which are generated by working people. To summarize, no matter what the direct source, ultimately all healthcare costs are derived from working-age earnings.

In table **1b**, we remove the 8% of health costs generated by children, as well as the $44 in revenue that is their portion of the $500 seed money, and redraw the graph; we move the beginning of the revenue curve to the time of birth, gaining three doublings of revenue. The anomalous excess of costs over revenues is reduced but not eliminated. The expected surplus appears as promised, but at the end of life, where it becomes considerably enhanced. The general financial idea is vindicated, but what of the children? Their costs are incorporated in an independent Health Savings Account. The legitimacy of doing so, and the financial consequences, are discussed in the following section. For the present, we can see from Figure 3a. that this approach helps but does not entirely reconcile the financing.

The revenue for that account is introduced at age 35 when health costs are predictably low, and ownership is transferred from the parents to the child. That is, we recognize the validity of such a transfer of responsibility, but during the transition from one system to the next, but must yield to the requirements of transition. Because of the overlaps, it may well be desirable to keep the two funds separate for quite a long time. It would seem premature to anticipate dynamic effects on the culture of marriage, divorce, and multiple family health insurance plans, and let the consolidation of accounts remain optional until much later in the unfolding of this scheme. Figure **1b** illustrates the effect of consolidating accounts in figure **5c,** and considerable experience with this issue probably exists within the life insurance industry. A reverse case can even be made for splitting the account into smaller age subgroups by logical age groups, as a way of easing the entanglements which people get themselves into.

http://www.philadelphia-reflections.com/blog/2798.htm

What I Have Learned (1)

This book has been an education for its author. Ordinarily, an author starts with a general principle, and offers a specific example of how it works. But I repeatedly found this field changed so quickly, changes in the numbers made the example seem awkward, if not invalid. Or one component changed, and balancing numbers were unobtainable. But I believe the underlying principles remain valid. It's better to earn interest on idle money than not to earn it, for example. But when the circumstances shift, the <u>amount</u> of interest to be earned – and consequently the proportion of healthcare costs it will cover – also shifts, allowing opponents to bring the underlying principle into doubt. When this process repeatedly leads to rewriting a whole book before it can be published, it essentially stifles debate. So I finally decided it was better to open the debate than worry about ridicule from hired political consultants over "framing the question", or protecting my offended feelings. At my age, what would I care about that, for heaven's sake?

So let's follow the trail of the book, and put together what I think I have learned, in the order in which it appears.

Pay for important things, first. Health insurance began a century ago, with good motives, but the wrong approach. It's upside down, in the sense that it started with the problems of poor people, and extended the approach to non-poor ones. Consequently, it offered "first dollar coverage" but threatened savings running out for truly expensive items, life-threatening ones. The most suitable way to get around this seems to be to have a high-deductible policy, which lets the patient decide what is truly most important. But two things then come in conflict: the higher the deductible, the lower the premium. That's good, but what's bad is the higher the deductible, the fewer people can afford it. So the Health Savings Account addressed this dilemma by linking high-deductible ("catastrophic") insurance to a tax-deductible savings account. In effect, the poor person could build up the deductible on time payments. It isn't perfect, but it was enough better so 15 million people adopted it, and their premiums became 30% lower. And so, more people could afford it.

Earn interest on savings. Then the patients taught me a lesson. In spite of abnormally low interest rates, people seemed to perceive that major illnesses come late in life, and longevity had lengthened considerably this century. And they liked the ability to judge their own health, letting the healthy ones pick stock investments if they chose to, because low interest rates shift many investors from bonds to stocks, which then rise. Sickly people could choose bonds, or tax-exempt savings accounts. Quite unique to American retirement funds, this one gave a second tax deduction when you spent it (if you spent it on health).

If there is money left over, you get to keep it. Conventional health insurance spent any left-over money to reduce premiums, they claimed. This one gave any money you saved back to you, as an incentive to be frugal. I suspect some people thought a bird in the hand was worth two in the bush, which means they didn't exactly trust insurance companies to lower premiums fully, but might have raised the salaries of insurance executives with some of the savings.

In time it developed a different significance: if you were lucky and healthy, you could spend the left-overs at age 66, for retirement income. The news about the approaching insolvency of Social Security encouraged that choice. At least, it began to look as though Social Security benefits might not be raised, so you might need the money more at a later time; compound interest made Health Savings Accounts worth more, later. Frugality early, led to more income later.

If anybody gets a tax deduction, everybody wants the same. For eighty years, employees of corporations got health insurance with a tax exemption, but half of the population didn't. That amounts yearly to a couple thousand dollars for a family, twice that much for the corporation itself (at its higher tax rates), and the possibility that even more escapes to foreign tax havens. By simply allowing the Health Savings Account to buy the catastrophic insurance which is required, this egregious inequity would disappear. If that gets blocked in Congress, then simply reduce the corporate tax rate, which corporations don't pay anyway because of the tax deduction. You might appear to be rewarding corporations, but you are really only shifting their deduction.

Save your deductions for later. It was a surprise to find 40% of subscribers to Health Savings Accounts paid for small health expenses out of pocket rather than take the tax deduction. It suddenly made sense that if the account would grow, and in any event you would get it back at age 66, you should pay out of pocket when it is small, saving the deduction until later when it had grown.

Split the payment system. Cash for outpatients, insurance for helpless inpatients. When you take away someone's clothes, and he is too sick in the hospital to argue, competitive prices are meaningless to him. Prices should be set by outpatients, who are free to trade elsewhere. A surprising number of inpatient services are identical to outpatient services, which should set the price for both. Some are unique, so a relative-value scale should be constructed to include them in the relationship.

Both the DRG system and co-payments are abominations. Payment by diagnosis is akin to service benefits, wrapped in a rationing system. Pay a fair fee for a necessary service, don't pay for an unnecessary one. As for copayment, it simplifies collective bargaining, but it creates two insurances for one service, and has been repeatedly shown to have no deterrence value.

Reverse the Maricopa Decision, preferably with legislation. Mrs. Clinton's plan of ten years ago was for a system of Health Maintenance Organizations (HMO). She can thank her lucky stars it didn't pass, because the public rejected them. HMOs were in fact invented by groups of doctors, and worked quite well. The essence of why they didn't work lies in the Maricopa decision that doctors were forbidden to run them. The Maricopa decision (4/3 on the Supreme Court) was based on a motion for summary judgment and never had a trial of the facts. Let's see if Congress can improve on that.

Substitute Catastrophic health insurance for any and all versions of limited benefits, including the Affordable Care Act. Catastrophic insurance is now privately run, and it is difficult to obtain data on costs and expenses. No doubt the plans vary considerably. But the system of indemnity insurance is superior to that of service benefits, and high deductible is superior to mandatory benefits. Catastrophic plans seem vulnerable to kickbacks, and should be examined to minimize that; perhaps I am wrong. Nevertheless, catastrophic was seemingly cheapest of what's available, and is certainly more flexible. If we must have mandatory health insurance – and I'm not saying we must – mandatory Catastrophic coverage sounds better than any alternative. But if we go that way, we need better studies of it.

http://www.philadelphia-reflections.com/blog/3468.htm

What I Have Learned (2)

That's what I believe I have learned from the Classical Health Savings Account of 1981, and what I think will improve it still further. Essentially, that's a correction of the tax inequity, a removal of the age restrictions to make it optional at any age, and an enlargement of the deposit limits. It requires very little legislation to accomplish those three things.

But my horizons have been expanded by the reception of the original, simple proposal. So I have some suggestions for Congress to consider, for a New HSA which is an extension of the classical variety. These ideas tend to bump into other programs and require negotiation of the apparent difficulties, with resultant adjustments of other plans, originally for other purposes.

Encourage the use of index funds as sources of investment income for HSAs In this era of abnormally low interest rates, the public seems to like the substitution of common stock, even though it seems risky. I'm afraid we have learned that bonds are just as risky. But they pay considerably less, except in rare moments of "black swan" recovery from a stock market crash. Roger Ibottson of Yale has published the long-term results of the entire stock market, which today we would equate with total market index funds. He found the results over the past century have averaged 11-12%. At a viewing distance of about three feet, regardless of many wars and stock crashes, if you had bought the whole market and forgot you had it, the average looks pretty much like a straight line. That's no guarantee it will be the same in the coming century, but it's the best guess you can make, particularly if you don't read the newspapers very often. Buy-and-hold almost becomes buy and forget.

That's the wrong risk to worry about, however. Inflation and imperfect agency are much greater risks for buy and hold. At 3% a year, inflation has reduced a dollar to a penny, in the past century. So, instead of 11-12 %, a buy-and-hold investor really only gets 8-9%, net of inflation. In addition to that, every 28-30 years he encounters a black swan stock market, loses at least 50%, and lacks the courage to buy it back at its low point. From that point forward, the market "climbs a wall of worry", and he finally buys it back just when it regains its peak.

The time-honored remedy is to buy a mixture of 60% stocks, 40% fixed income (bonds), which reduces real income to 4-6%. If we ever cure this habit, gross stock prices will probably gravitate toward paying 5-7%, gross. Unfortunately, middle-man fees and kickbacks result in the customer getting 4-6%, trying to avoid getting zero. Unfortunately, the majority of experts actually surrender somewhat less than that, and the reasonable investor simply buys index funds and forgets about them. That is, it comes out about the same, unless you get greedy, in which case most people end up losing money. For the most part, whether you win or lose, mostly has to do with where the market was when you started.

Consequently, we here advise "passive" investing, in an index mixture of total American stocks and bonds. You will do better than most people, and that's a pretty good badge of success. However, the puzzle is whether rules and regulations can improve on this result, by a tenth of a percent, here and there. Those who promise more, will probably deliver less.

Stretch out the compound interest as long as possible. Since Aristotle, it has always surprised people to find compound interest rises at the end of its term, so the longer the better is the best theory. We make three suggestions:

1. **Don't buy term insurance (like most health insurance), buy whole-life.** You might turn the whole business over to whole-life life insurance companies with experience in these matters, but they are private companies who can do as they please. The next-best choice is a Health Savings Account, which rolls any unspent balance over to later years, and gives it back to you at age 66. It's tax-exempt, and if you spend it on healthcare, it is doubly so.

2. **Use last year of life re-insurance.** People die at different ages, but the last year is usually the most costly, and it happens to everyone. If you set aside a comparatively small amount of money at birth, it will multiply 289 times at 6.5%, by the age of 84, the current average longevity. If it is transferred to Medicare, it reduces Medicare costs by at least a quarter, and Medicare really should refund a quarter of your payroll deductions as well as your Medicare premiums, maybe even more. The arithmetic is pretty complicated, but with luck it might pay for all of Medicare, except for existing debts for borrowing earlier when we ran a deficit. Furthermore. Medicare is 50% subsidized, so that has to be figured, too. Extending this subsidy to everyone is a big argument against single payer, by the way.

3. **Use first year of life reinsurance.** This is the reverse of the above, because the 3% of healthcare costs now thought to affect newborns is almost invariably donated by

another generation. Young parents without much savings are strained to subsidize their children, so you might as well include children to the age of 21, which is 8% of healthcare costs. If you overfund Medicare by $100 at birth, it will grow by enough to subsidize grandchildren by the time grandpa dies. There are laws against perpetuities, but they limit inheritances to one lifetime, plus 21 years – plenty of time. This is a new concept which will take time to adjust to, but I can think of no other way to pre-pay a newborn infant. If you use some variant of this approach, health costs could be reduced by another 8%, for a cost of less than $100.

In closing, let me remind the reader health insurance is turning into a gigantic transfer system. The middle third of life is supporting the two-thirds, before and after. And only the last third has much sickness. People who are well don't like to subsidize those who are sick, and eventually may rebel. It's much better for young individuals to subsidize their own old age, than for one demographic group to subsidize another group of strangers. Particularly if those few who are lucky and escape much sickness, get to keep the savings for their protracted retirement.

http://www.philadelphia-reflections.com/blog/3469.htm